THE SPIRIT OF GLASSBORO

& OTHER TALES OF TERROR

BY ANDREW KRAUS

The Spirit of Glassboro & Other Tales of Terror

Copyright © 2018 by Andrew Kraus

White Sands by Andrew Kraus Copyright © 2018

ISBN: 9781980842149

Illustrations and cover by Nathan Davis

Follow Andrew on Twitter: @AndyK1005

DEDICATION

Early on, I had a passion for writing. My first stories included tales about a raisin who came to life from a box of cereal. Based on a popular dried grape singing troupe brought to life thanks to the art of Claymation, my little raisin friend named Crazy took me on many adventures. As I grew older, my stories included the adventures of Bunny Bear and Aardvark, based on my son's plush friends. Throughout my writing, whether my work was read by close friends and family or strangers who found them interesting, I always envisioned one person being there to see me follow through on a childhood dream.

A teacher I had the opportunity to know throughout high school, Mrs. Dana DiPerna Pillsbury, was a teacher who inspired not just me, but a generation of children in an east coast Florida town. Back when Oprah was on TV, I'd imagine being interviewed by her with Dana sitting in the front row.

As life happens with college, marriage, children and work, I lost touch with Dana. One day, a few years ago, I finally reconnected with her thanks to the power of social media. I had the opportunity to let her know how much a five-foot woman influenced the life of a six-foot and two-inch man.

When we reconnected, as many of my high school classmates did with her, I learned that she had been battling an aggressive form of breast cancer. Her social media posts were always inspiring and smart, never complaining. An artist friend of hers painted Dana on a hillside, standing on the second rung of a ladder, reaching for the moon.

Upon returning from a long vacation in Europe, I came home to learn that Dana had lost her battle with cancer. The news hit me like a ton of bricks. I missed an opportunity to follow my dreams and dedicate my first book to her. My daydream of seeing her smile as she opened a box that contained my book, signed on the page dedicated to her, was dashed.

Teachers are more influential and impactful than we sometimes realize, especially when they are an awe inspiring and formidable force like Mrs. Dana DiPerna Pillsbury. No matter if one person reads this book or a thousand, I wrote this book for myself and in honor of a wonderful teacher, friend and person.

With angel wings and free from any pain, I hope she was able to hug the moon at last. Never forgotten and always with me. Thank you, Dana.

ACKNOWLEDGEMENTS

It takes perseverance, hard work, and a little "Daddy Andy" juice never hurts, to write a book. There is no way I could have made this dream of mine come true without the help of close friends and family along the way.

Thank you to Elanna Grant for helping me get this book into print. Thank you to Nate Davis for creating a beautiful and haunting image on the cover of this book. I truly appreciate your tireless effort and help.

To my fears and tiny moments in everyday life, thank you for inspiring each chapter and the drama each character faces. To each of my phobias, worries or dark thoughts- thank you.

My dear Ethan, I couldn't have asked for a better son. A budding writer himself, we spent many afternoons and late evenings writing stories together. I hope someday the world will embrace his story about the haunted woods.

Last, but by far not the least, thank you to my husband Chris. Without you, this book would never have come to fruition. You painstakingly proofread each chapter again and again to fix grammar and typos. You motivated me to get my butt off the couch and turn off reruns of the Golden Girls to get upstairs and write. Without your love and support, this book would never have been possible. From the day we met, you've been there for me no matter what and this middle-aged person with moderate self-esteem thanks you. With three squeezes, my love is infinite.

P.S. To the ghosts that inhabit our home, thank you for allowing me to tell your stories.

TABLE OF MACABRE CONTENTS

FOREWORD

Holding a steaming bowl of macaroni and cheese while watching classic movies under a warm blanket on a rainy day can be as satisfying as reading a scary story. Comforted by the misery of others and often left without ample time to soak in never-ending four-hundred-page tales, a good short story can do the trick.

After reading several long-winded novels with the most interesting parts found somewhere in the back of chapter thirteen, I found myself craving just the juicy details, the heart of the story. I didn't care what shade of blue the curtains were or what brands of perfume and products adorned a dresser. Let's just get to the hacking, stalking, scaring, sad, gross, turn my eyes away for a moment-type pages otherwise known as the good parts. When I read Stephen King's Thinner, a good book but not such a good movie, I remember the page that described a character's acne curse. King went into major detail mode about the character's face covered in bubbling pimple blisters and what happened to each puss-filled capsule as the person slowly scratched their cheek. God was that a good page. It was the reason why I enjoyed the book so much. I remember turning the page with just the tips of my fingers, as though the ooze from the character's face had permeated the page and my world inside my college dorm room.

I often find myself watching the six o'clock and six-thirty news waiting for that teaser story about the item under my kitchen sink that will sure kill me. I'd sit through the stories about politics, crime and even the "make you feel all fuzzy inside" story about a kid and a puppy or what a cute sea lion did on the beach. And then finally, the story I had been waiting for, the moment building for an hour and then the feeling of defeat to learn the killer product under my sink could have only been purchased in a store we don't have anywhere near my state and it hadn't been on the market in over five years. Again, wait for the good stuff and like a child begging for a balloon at an amusement park, I was only satisfied for a few fleeting moments.

In our busy lives, our time is often controlled by work and family schedules. Who has time to read though four hundred pages just to find out the good parts were just really ten pages? I don't know about most people, but my own time, the time just for me and not the rest of the world, can only really be found in one place- the bathroom. And except for the one time we ate bad shrimp from the grocery store at a summer party, who can spend enough time on the porcelain bowl to read an entire book?

Short stories, for me anyway, can focus on the details, the point. The parts of the character's lives that really matter to the reader. I don't want to see John Doe buy milk from the pantry store. I just want to see the part of his story where he's running for his life with the Boogey Man just ten steps behind. Even close friends, co-workers and family members, no matter how much they think they know us, only really get a small glimpse into our lives. So then why does a reader get the right to know everything about a character in a book? Unless I'm reading about a biography or their past is integral to the story, who gives a whoop.

When light flashes across my bedroom ceiling, or an orb huddles over my child's crib, or invisible fists pound down hard on our piano, we don't then hear the ghosts give the reason why. Living in a house with a few humans, both from this world and beyond, we are often left with the action and reaction from our spirited companions but rarely ever the reasons why. Well, except the one time the former owner died and her children wanted to pay a visit to check out our home. We were not available to let them in and we ended up spending the night chasing down smoke alarms ringing throughout the night on each floor. Lesson learned. Never anger the recently departed. It's polite to let them cross over, at least out of the neighborhood.

Motivated by ghosts, encouraged by my family and inspired by things that go bump in the night, I was driven to write these short stories based on fears and curiosities we all face. When we pass a white van on the highway with the windows painted over, what do you assume is in the back? Plumbing supplies, electrical parts, or the kidnapped victim announced in an emergency broadcast. When you are alone stirring meatballs on the stove and you feel something gently touch the back of your neck, do you think it was just the air conditioning, a spirit, or possibly the tiny legs from a poisonous hairy spider repelling down toward you from the ceiling and landing on the inside of your shirt collar. Out of respect for time and my own personal interest in things I find exciting, I focus on the spider angle, leaving out the meatball prep from the story. I could dive into the details of adding the mixture of beef, pork and veal into a bowl, then breadcrumbs, seasoning, egg and milk but I'm not looking to read a cook book. I want to hear the details that send shivers down my spine, goosebumps up my arms and question whether I am alone in the room. Alone being a relative term of course as someone could be watching us in our comfortable vulnerable state from a window or stand over our shoulder in a physical-free form. Did you just brush your collar to shoo away an invisible spider?

Ghost stories and thrilling tales don't have to be reserved for a camp fire or a dark and stormy night. The adrenal rush of reading something hauntingly too close to home can leave us satisfied and grateful that it was him and not me. Her and not you. Them and not us. But are we all just in our own short horror story with someone reading along, turning the pages of our lives?

With spirited eagerness and devilish anticipation, I hope you enjoy these short stories and tales, written to thrill and cause a few chills.

THE SPIRIT OF GLASSBORO

The summer of 1967 would transform the small peaceful New Jersey town and its residents forever, leaving them terrified by a legend that would haunt them for years to come.

In late June, President Lyndon B. Johnson met with Alexei Kosygin, the Premier of the Soviet Union in an unlikely United States location. Glassboro, New Jersey served as the ideal backdrop for this diplomatic encounter, far enough from Vietnam War protestors in New York and away from the spotlight of Washington, DC. The world leaders met at Hollybush Mansion on the campus at the then Glassboro State College, hoping to improve relations between their two countries.

On the eve of the third and final day of the conference, something went terribly wrong. One of the leaders of the Soviet Political Bureau was found dead in his room. Most of the skin from his body shredded, he lay in a pool of blood and mangled bowels. His teeth were strewn across the Venetian rug, some clinging on to bits of root and gum-line. A large travel trunk at the base of the bed was lying open on its side. Something had escaped the trunk by clawing and eating its way out. The corner of the trunk lid ripped away, peeled away like a small bomb exploded inside. Blood and a patch of long black hair clung to the carnage of twisted metal. Whatever was inside the trunk had escaped by crashing through the third-floor window, disappearing into the night of the small, factory town.

Speculation ran rampant as to what was in the trunk and who put it in there. Was it militants from Vietnam, hoping to stop a union between the U.S. and Soviet Union or nationalists from the Arab States or Israel, trying to draw in the nations of power into their war?

The conference abruptly ended the following morning on June 25th, toted as a success by the media, referring to the summit as the "Spirit of Glassboro." Little did they know that a spirit, an unimaginable beast, was just unleashed, hungry, on the small New Jersey town.

Since the late 1700's, Glassboro prospered to become one of the nation's leading glass-making towns. Still led by the bloodlines of the Whitney and Stanger families, the large factory in the center of town produced window glass, bottles and hollowware. The two leading families, and their abundance of wealthy offspring, lived in the large manor homes that surrounded Glen Lake while the factory's workers and journeymen lived in the uniform and small homes of the Carpenter and Bowman neighborhoods, much less affluent in many ways. In the months following the summit, rumors and whispers of strange sightings ran rampant throughout the houses of Carpenter and Bowman. The teeth of rabbits, wild animals and most often, cats, had been found in the streets and along the town's main road to the factory. The bodies of the victims were never found, only the teeth were left behind.

As the sun sank below the horizon each evening, the factory fires burned into the night sky, setting an orange, protective glow around the workspace. The surrounding neighborhoods seemed darker, tucked into the shadows of the night and away from the glow of the factory. Glass was produced around the clock. As the families around Glen Lake sat down for their dinner feasts, the town's workers traded positions and the night shift began. Often, both mothers and fathers worked at the glass factory, leaving their children home alone at night, protected only by a locked front door.

At first, most of the missing children were from the Whitney and Stanger neighborhoods. The frantic panic-stricken parents searched and cried out to the wealthy, police and government families of Glen Lake, often on deaf ears, only to be told that their children ran away in search of better lives, better families.

Month after month, glass production continued and more and more children disappeared, snatched away in the middle of the night. The only evidence left behind in their beds was a tattered sheet and blood-stained teeth on the bedroom windowsill, the window always forced open from the outside.

It wasn't until an unseasonably warm evening in late October, that the matter of missing children was taken seriously by the well-to-do. Jeramiah Stanger and his wife Elizabeth, held a harvest ball, inviting only Glassboro's elite. Upon returning home after an evening of dancing and drinking wine out of their locally produced glass works, Thomas and Gayle Whitney found their children's nanny dead on the ground in front of the nursery's fireplace, her throat had been slashed. The large bay windows stretched out toward the night sky and the children's beds were empty. Edward and Peter were nowhere to be found, only a few small teeth were left behind on the mattresses. A tuft of long black hair clung to a corner of the windowsill.

The police took the case at once and made finding the children and the perpetrator a top priority. The glass factory ran business as usual and to protect their remaining children, the working mothers and fathers left their children in the care of neighbors who worked the day shift and, in return, the neighbors would have their children watched by others when they went to work. The window glass they made was not strong enough to protect their children from the creature that feasted at night. Shutters were closed, often reinforced with boards nailed on top one another.

Against their best efforts, the police could not locate the missing boys and more and more children disappeared. The light of day revealed splintered wood, missing children, empty beds and of course, teeth.

As more children disappeared, family after family fled Glassboro and soon, the orange light that lit up the night sky from the factory was snuffed out. The factory produced only during the day and the emotional and financial impact took its toll. Frequent deliveries of high-end meats and fashion goods from New York City all but stopped to the homes along Glen Lake. Each night, parents stayed home to protect their children the best they could.

A Nor'easter blew in ferociously in early January and the remaining residents of Glassboro found themselves sheltered close to home, buried in snow and a hard, long freeze. The factory shut down and to their relief and gratitude, children stopped disappearing.

Some of the Whitney and Stanger families moved to New York City and Charleston. Thomas Whitney and Jeramiah Stanger's families were the last to live along Glen Lake, in large white, three-story manors across the street from one another. To find another source of income, they sold most of the surrounding land to farmers who planted crops of onion and asparagus.

Thomas and Gayle Whitney refused to leave their home, desperate and hopeful that one day their lost boys would return to them. The factory was sold to Riley Carpenter who instead of producing bottles and window glass, produced jars for whiskey and rye.

Many of the residents fled Glassboro but the few that remained, believed the harsh winter killed the creature that terrorized them, unable to survive in the freezing temperature.

The Whitney family died in their home a few years later. After sitting vacant for three years, one of the farmers purchased the home, moving his wife, two daughters and three sons into the stately old manor.

The Stanger's left their home and moved to Charleston to be near their children and never returned.

Since the winter of 1968, there had only been a few rumblings of sightings of the creature. The Glassboro History Museum displayed a wooden shutter with four long marks stretched across the grain. Some people say it was a fake, carvings made by a knife or a pitchfork to frighten children, done to keep them in line at night to guard against mischief and pranks.

Eventually, the homes in the town's Carpenter and Bowman neighborhoods were razed to make way for an extension of Glassboro State College.

As more and more construction on the new college continued, pieces of broken glass were unearthed around the site, often piercing the boots of workers. Farmers around Glen Lake also found bits of glass mixed among the growing asparagus and onion. Before pouring the foundation of a new wing at the college, workers unearthed teeth, at first paying no attention to them, thinking they were remains of animals.

With the growth of the school and thanks to an urban renewal project to revamp the main street area, Glassboro flourished. The farmers around Glen Lake were forced out to neighboring towns and new homes popped up close to the old great manors.

Residents still find glass in their yards to this day, and occasionally find teeth. Could they be the teeth from the missing children or teeth from an animal long rotted away? Faint cries in the woods near Glen Lake late at night are often heard. The sound much like that of a wounded puppy or heartbroken cat, fill the sky on warm, summer evenings. Some ignore the cries and believe the noise is likely from a loud neighbor across the way but those residents who survived, those residents that know the teeth they find are the teeth of children, know better.

They know the Spirit of Glassboro has not truly gone away. It waits, somewhere in the dark, to return and feast on a new generation of children.

DELL FISHER

It was the perfect day for a drive. Dell Fisher cruised down the long highway in his '89 Ford cab pick-up truck. The sun had just begun to peak over the horizon and its golden rays illuminated the barren forest that hugged the narrow two-lane road. The morning frost melted and dripped off the body of the faded cream-colored car, disappearing as each drop took flight above the pavement.

Dell adjusted the front windshield defogger on his dashboard and then settled back, deep into his seat. He felt surprised that his hands were not too sweaty inside his leather gloves. He had the gloves for almost as long as he had his Ford. The leather cracked and bits of camel-colored stuffing snuck out between some of the fingertips. They were his favorite gloves. For a moment, Dell took his eyes off the highway and stared at his gloves as he squeezed the steering wheel and flexed his fingers. *Good gloves*, he thought. These gloves were with him when he shot the large buck last November from his secret tree post near his cabin in the woods. It was unseasonably colder that day, much like today. He knew he would have lost his fingers to frostbite waiting for that buck to cross his path if it hadn't been for these gloves. *Good gloves,* he thought again.

He looked up into the rear-view mirror and noticed the highway was still empty, not a car in sight. It was, after all, about 6:30am Thanksgiving morning and most of the travelers along Highway 43 had reached their final destinations the night before. Most people would be asleep after a long day in heavy traffic and only a handful would be waking up to begin preparing for the holiday dinner. Growing up in Martin Falls, Dell knew that this stretch of road was mainly traveled by locals and only around the holidays did it see its fair share of traffic; the residents of Martin Falls sharing this shortcut from the interstate with their loved ones.

Dell adjusted the rear-view mirror and tilted it to get a good look at the back seat. His wife Miriam was bundled up across the seat and she hadn't moved. He cleared his throat and aimed the mirror back on the road behind him. Still empty.

He could hardly believe that it had been a year already since he shot that Buck, the years flying by faster and faster ever since he turned sixty. He and his wife had been together off and on for about thirty years. She was his second wife. His first wife Lucy had been his high school sweetheart and they had a son together, Patrick. Once Patrick went away to college, Dell learned that his wife was having an affair with one of the hands on their farm and shortly after that, she and her lover disappeared.

It took Dell a few years to trust women again like he did his gloves and a good, ice cold Coors Light. Miriam was a regular at his usual bar hangout and it took about a year for her to move in. Not being able to legally re-marry since Lucy vanished with her beau, Miriam and Dell had their own unofficial wedding ceremony with a few friends in their new home and considered themselves as good as married. Miriam figured that if two men could consider themselves married without being official from the state, then why couldn't they? There was no way Dell was going to live at the Farm of Adultery, as he called it, so he sold the farm and bought a small home on the outskirts of town near Johnson's Bridge.

He loved Miriam but after being cheated on by his first wife, there was always a bit of doubt left inside him. Most people found Dell off-putting and a tad grumpy but he knew it was because he mainly kept to himself. Again, Dell adjusted himself in the front seat of the car as he thought about the people he and Miriam called friends and neighbors. He didn't have many friends, mainly drinking buddies that lined the bar with rows of half-drunken Coors Lites, stale pretzels in old wooden bowls and the sound of a football game on the TV above the shelf of Jack Daniels, Jim Bean and Wild Turkey. It was a good bar; dark and everyone minded their own business. You came in for a drink and a game and left conversation at the door. At home, Miriam did enough talking for the both of them.

In the beginning, Dell thought he had found another good companion in Miriam like he had in Lucy but shortly after moving in and getting unlawfully hitched, he learned just how chatty she was. She talked in the morning as she made his eggs and scrapple, she talked over lunch while making tuna fish, she talked while doing laundry and the talking continued through dinner until she fell asleep beside him in bed. She would engage him for opinions about her friends, about what she read in the latest edition of Women's Circle or about something she learned on a show on the TV. He would grunt and agree and quickly learned if he had an opinion that differed from hers that the conversation would just drag on longer and longer.

Dell tilted his head from shoulder to shoulder to stretch out his neck. He looked in the mirror again and still no cars were coming in either direction.

He wondered if she had always been so talkative. Had he never noticed when they met in the bar? Had talking been a two-way street for them or was it always just her gabbing on and on and him just waiting for what usually happened at the end of the date, a relief from the day's tension. Dell wasn't the most passionate of lovers. He knew that. To him, the act of sex was much like riding his old tractor through the field of soy at his old farm- the tractor took a long time to get started and heated up but once it got going, Dell couldn't wait to plow through the work and get to the cold Coors Lite waiting for him back in the cooler at the barn. It was all just work to him, whether he had on his overalls and dependable leather gloves in the field or when he had to drop trough and satisfy the urges of wife and himself after a late night of TV news. He was happy that he at least got to keep his socks on during it all. He thought there was nothing worse than rubbing against Miriam's legs when she skipped a day or two shaving them. The stubble reminded him of those prickly wild raspberry bushes near his cabin. He ripped those bushes out of the ground as soon as he inherited the cabin from his father. He knew he may not have been the ideal husband, but at least he was faithful and to him, that is all that mattered.

The gas gauge read half a tank and he was driving at a steady 55mph. The sun rose higher into the clear sky, flickering between the trees like a never-ending camera flash. Dell adjusted the driver-side visor and slid it over the side window to block out the light. He turned his head for another peak at Miriam, still out.

He began to think about all the work he had to do once he got back home. This Thanksgiving, he was not going to eat turkey like every other schmoe in the country. He was saving a nice big piece of that buck in the freezer for a special occasion and today was surely it. The loin was his favorite part and later he would be enjoying it at a peaceful holiday dinner with yams, canned peas, a Coors Lite, and the apple pie Miriam bought yesterday from the grocery store.

Dell glanced back in the rear-view mirror for a moment and expected to see nothing. Instead, he was startled at the sight of a car racing up the highway behind him. He squinted to get a better look and, as the car got closer, the square glob came into focus. He could clearly see the outline of police lights on the road. It was a local sheriff's car. Dell looked back at Miriam. She was still flat against the backseat. He turned his head and focused on the road, maintaining a nice pace of 55mph. The sheriff's car raced up behind him quickly, then moved into the empty oncoming lane of traffic and sped by him. It disappeared ahead of him just as quickly as it had appeared behind him. Dell exhaled and flexed his fingers again against the steering wheel. *Good gloves*, he thought.

The turn-off for his cabin was coming up. Just a few miles more and he would be on a side road, private and closer to his cabin. The road was unpaved and quite a bit bumpy. Large potholes and the occasional small branches lined his path. He could see the trees giving way just ahead on the right and he slowed the Ford down to 15mph as he turned onto the dirt road. Because it had been a cold, rainy weekend leading up to this clear morning, the dust and dirt remained on the road and it did not cloud up along the sides of his truck. Keeping at a speed of 15mph, the truck still bounced and flopped along the uneven road. Miriam slid a little on the backseat and Dell could hear the metal from his shovel and tools slide around the metallic truck bed. He knew he had only a few more miles on this road to go until he'd reach the cabin.

Patrick had decided not to come home for Thanksgiving this year. He called his dad last weekend to say that he, his wife and their two young kids were going to spend the holiday with his wife's family. He promised Dell that they would be with him for Christmas and they even invited Dell and Miriam to join them. Spending a holiday with the in-laws at their upstate New York condo was not the ideal setting for Dell. He preferred his quiet, hometown in Virginia. He loved Patrick and his wife wasn't half-bad. The children though, four and six years old, were an absolute nightmare. Dell never had a soft spot for children and even though these two were his grandkids, his own flesh and blood, he thought they acted like two wild boars, knocking over everything in his house with a unquenching hunger for more and more cheddar crackers shaped like tiny fish. Crushed-up bits of orange dust would linger all year long in the shag carpet alongside the pine needles from former Christmas trees.

Yes, let the in-laws enjoy the little beasts. Dell had other plans and intended to enjoy this Thanksgiving in peace.

Dell could see the cabin just ahead and he slowed even more as he parked alongside it and a large rusted white tank that once held heating oil. Dell had given up on getting an oil truck out there to fill it up. He thought it wasn't worth the hassle or the price so for the last several years, he heated up the cabin by keeping a roaring fire going in the old stone fireplace. Miriam found it cold and drafty and she didn't like coming to the cabin if it wasn't summer time. Dell thought that was just fine and went there often to hunt and for necessary isolation.

Dell turned the keys in the ignition to the off position and the engine of the reliable old Ford shuttered to a quiet still. He turned to the back seat and leaned over, giving Miriam a good hard poke with one of the keys. She didn't budge.

He opened his door and climbed out the car and then opened the cab's backseat passenger door and took a long hard look at his wife. She lay motionless on the seat, wrapped tightly in a clear plastic tarp. The large tarp wound around her small body several times. He could see the top of her much-greyed red hair through the opened end of the plastic cocoon.

Dell reached in and grabbed a hold of the tarp and gave it a good strong pull. Her body slid out of the car and onto the dirt driveway. He closed the truck doors and looked down at the tarp. He could see the blue from her jeans and the flannel pattern from her shirt through the layers of plastic. Blood had smeared around the area near her head and the tarp did well to contain it. The frozen buck shank would sure serve him well later. He thought about the shank and how satisfying it was going to taste, alongside the yams, canned peas, a cold Coors Lite and the pie that Miriam had gotten from the grocery store yesterday.

He also thought about the day when he came home to find a strange blue car in his driveway. He parked his truck in the street, snuck up to the house and watched through the bedroom window while the bodies of Miriam and a naked man bounced up and down on his bed sheets like a child's teeter totter.

There was no other course of action for Dell than to help Miriam and her lover disappear, much like how he had assisted Lucy and her beau. Nothing was worse than being unfaithful. Death, being alone or engaging in short banter at the bar over a beer did not compare to the feeling of being cheated on. Miriam should have known better, he thought. He thought she also should have known better to duck when a frozen solid buck shank is swinging toward her skull.

Dell reached into the bed of his truck and removed the shovel. With his other hand, he bent down and grabbed a good piece of the tarp's edge and dragged Miriam into the woods. The brown leaves crunched under his foot and the wrapped-up tarp slid along the trail. Dell knew the woods like the many cracks in his favorite gloves. He had just been up to the cabin yesterday while Miriam was shopping at the grocery store. He followed his own path to a small clearing of trees. He let go of the tarp and moved to the center of the clearing. Dell held the shovel with two hands and began to dig through the leaves until he found what he was looking for. A corner of a wood plank stuck out from the leaves and he dropped the shovel. He bent over and slid the plank to one side, grabbed a hold of three more planks of wood and slid them out of the way as well. A large hole revealed itself. It was a dried up old well that used to supply water to the cabin. For years now, Dell had to bring plastic gallon jugs of water to the cabin for bathing and cooking. The outhouse served its purpose for relieving his body of urine and his morning constitution.

Dell tossed the shovel onto the ground and looked back at Miriam's wrapped body. He left her on the ground and walked back to the cabin, unlocked the door and stepped inside, leaving the front door open. He appeared back on the old wooden porch and dragged out another body wrapped in plastic. This body was much heavier and Dell noticed the blood smeared in small circular swirls around the person's back. He learned that he could take down a buck just as efficiently as he could a man.

He didn't say anything as he dragged the body to the well. He was much heavier than Miriam and each time Dell exhaled, a cloud of fog escaped his mouth and the cold, crisp air made him appear like an old smoking steam engine.

Dell slid the body of the man to the well and pushed it in and watched as the plastic tarp and its contents disappeared down into darkness. He then turned to the body of his unlawfully wedded wife and she too joined her lover down into darkness. He stared into the well for a moment and wiped his nose with his glove. The coldness and the bit of heavy lifting had caused his nose to begin to run. Dell then slid the planks back over the hole and used the shovel to stir around the leaves, camouflaging the well again.

Dell closed the front door to his cabin, tossed the shovel into the truck bed and climbed back into his old Ford. The old reliable engine started and he put the truck in reverse. He placed a hand along the seat beside him and began to back the truck up. He looked at his gloved hand on the seat and flexed his fingers. *Good gloves*, he said.

He drove slowly down the dirt road toward Highway 43 and headed for home to prepare his peaceful holiday dinner of buck shank, yams, canned-peas, a Coors Lite and the apple pie Miriam bought at the grocery store yesterday.

SERIAL AM I

Give me some rest

I feel so old

My blood is drained

Turning me cold

-Voivod

To kill. To murder. To take a life. Have you ever? Do you know what it feels like to hold a heart as it rhythmically slows until it no longer beats? Do you know how it feels to thrust your hands into a pool of warm blood and feel the temperature gradually cool? Colder and colder it gets. Thicker and thicker, like a pot of pasta sauce on the stove. Burner off- forever. Slowly cools but forever staining your hands.

No, not a hunter deep in the woods in search of a helpless deer. Never a coward like that, hiding in the brush or in a makeshift nest in the tree waiting for his prey. Not a soldier on a battlefield, shooting to kill or to be killed for God and his country, hiding in the trenches.

I don't hide. I am out in the open behind you at the grocery checkout line, in the car next to you in that traffic jam yesterday and invited to your child's birthday party. I am the one wearing the paper, coned-birthday cap and eating cake next to your family. I am behind you and your best friend at the cinema. You, watching the movie and me, watching you. I watch everyone around me.

Who will be next? Whose life will end by the power of my hands and by the power of my knife? The birthday clown that didn't make you laugh? The movie theater attendant who overcharged you for popcorn? The driver in the car in front of me in traffic who always stops short or lets every other car into our lane? My knife cautiously slides through the chest wall between the bones, moving in deeper like cutting the perfect slice of cake. My victim's blood escaping and covering my hand the deeper and deeper I go with the eyes, once big and round with surprise and fear, slowly closing. The tension in the body gone forever. My sweet victory.

I must dive into you deeply and feel you go. Not a killer. Not a murderer. Not a hunter. I am a survivor and I must end your life to survive.

I am like the jolly fat elf who creeps down your chimney or the winged beast who reaches under your pillow while you sleep to steal your teeth. I can be anywhere, everywhere, and no one will know until they take the first of their finals breaths.

At first, I'd kill by the usual methods like stabbing with a kitchen knife, thrusting an ice pick into the eye socket and then through the brain and once I had to carve a body like a Thanksgiving turkey with a chainsaw. Unfortunately, none of those methods were ever truly satisfying. Suddenly like a stroke of genius, a life-altering spark hit me one day while I had a young woman tied to a chair. I was about to slit her throat with a corkscrew I found in her house when something struck me, literally. It was one of her cats. I looked down and saw a grey, short-haired feline rubbing its body back and forth on my pant leg. I looked up at the restrained girl to tell her that her cat would die first but then I saw another cat jump up onto the couch cushion behind her, then another one. She had three cats.

The corkscrew in my hand felt like a foreign object. I placed the spiraled metal opener back down on the coffee table. I turned and walked into the kitchen and opened each cupboard until I found what I was instinctively looking for- cat food. Cans and cans of cat food were piled up high on a shelf. I grabbed one, Tuna Medley, and searched for a can opener. An electric open was mounted under one of the cabinets and I attached the lid to the magnetic piece of the can opener and pressed the power button. The can slowly spun as the opener groaned. The lid popped up more and more as it spun around until it finally detached from the bottom of the can. I threw the bottom of the can on the kitchen floor and Tuna Medley spilled out across the tile. The three cats came running and began slurping up their new feast.

I reached over and removed the can's lid from the opener and brought it close to my eye for inspection. The razor-sharp edges would surely do the trick. How much fun this was going to be to slice the girl up, bit by bit, with something she associates with love and kindness.

I held onto the lid as though it were a playing card I was about to toss. It felt good between my fingers. It felt right.

The girl wriggled in her restraints as I approached her. She cried and tried to scream through the mouth gag but it was no use. No one could hear her except for me and her cats.

With one hand, I squeezed her cheeks until she was forced to stick out her tongue. I then held on tight to the tip and she wriggled and tried to loosen my grip. Gingerly, I slid the edge of the cat food lid across her tongue, from as far back as I could reach in her mouth to the very tip of it. She cried out in pain as the blood oozed out like lava from an erupting volcano. I let go and it snapped back into her mouth, blood pouring down her throat and choking her. She gagged and cried, unable to scream out, choking on her own blood. The sour seafood smell from the lid intertwined with the aroma of iron.

I watched her for a moment and didn't think that this was the way this girl should die.

With my left hand, I grabbed her by the back of the hair and slowly pulled her head back to reveal her smooth, pasty-white neck. With my right hand, I gently slid the edge of the lid against her neck, slicing through her skin and digging a little deeper in as I went. Her gargled cries quickly changed to a muffled, gasping sound as the life in her body slowly drained away. Her blood raced down her neck and more poured down to her lungs, her red bouquet soaked her blouse.

She stopped gagging and wriggling and her body stopped writhing. Her head dropped toward her bosom, dead.

What a splendid experience it was. The sensation of the crude blade slicing through her tongue, the warm sensation of her blood comforting my fingers as they swept across her throat and the unexpected grand finale of the cats drinking from the blood that pooled just beneath her.

My work was truly an art form. How clever I was to use the lid of the can and how thoughtful of her to supply the mechanism of her own demise.

While in search of my greatest masterpiece, there were several works of art along the way like the house cleaner who was left alone on a chilly November morning. I hid behind the couch, waiting for her to take a break at 10:45 like she usually did. Just as she relaxed back on the couch, I thrust the broomstick through the cushion and I'll never forget the sensation of the splintered wooden spear as it pierced the skin of her back and leapt forward out through her chest. Astonished at what just happened to her, she looked down and gripped the broomstick with both hands. She tried to pull it out but she had no idea the plastic bristle head was still attached and too bulky to slip through the back of the couch and out through the front of her body.

I stood up from behind the couch, and she raised her eyes only once to see who did this awful thing to her. With a few stuttered gargles of choking blood, she died.

Some people enjoy the sounds of a cooing baby, of waves crashing on the beach or of raindrops against a windowpane. I personally enjoy the soothing gurgling sound of blood percolating up the back of the throat as a person struggles to catch a final breath. The sound reminds me of a brook, roaring through snow-covered ice where the brilliant freshly laid powder is contrary to the warm crimson gore melting to the ground below from my latest kill.

Over the past few years, there have been countless people who have surrendered their lives to me so I can survive in your world. There are definitely a few honorable mentions like the man who changed lanes on the interstate and almost took off my car's front bumper. I caught up with him at a gas station bathroom where he had an unfortunate encounter with a dirty toilet bowl and the lid of its porcelain tank. His head severed from his body and left in the bowl as a surprise for the next patron. I noted how long it took to sever the spine and break through his neck muscles by using the lid. It was a lot of work, very worth the outcome but I knew I would have enjoyed it more if I could have savored the moment.

The more lives I took, the emptier I became. Something was missing. I began to feel like an over-eater who gorged himself on chocolate cookie cream sandwiches and jars of peanut butter. Sure, the cookies and peanut butter tasted good going down and satisfied my cravings temporarily, but as soon as the box was empty, the hunger inside me continued, relentlessly.

I was an addict wanting more and more and I saw no end in sight. No light at the end of the tunnel. I thought I would spend eternity taking lives, temporarily basking in pools of blood and clever ways to bring on death.

Then, as though struck with a thunderbolt, it hit me. I had just killed a set of roommates, two college-aged kids home for an intimate evening, never knowing that one would die by having their limbs slowly ground through the garbage disposal and the other choke on a cocktail of Draino and Clorox Bleach, the acid burning through his esophagus and exploding out his mouth like an erupting volcano. It was then, in the final moments of forcing the elbow through the disposal, that I realized what my life's work was all about, who I had been doing this for.

Unlike most kids who endured years of embarrassing hugs at school plays by mommy and daddy or an overabundance of presents on Christmas morning, my parents enjoyed showering me with hot scalding water and beating me in the basement with two by fours. Each special event, whether birthday, Christmas or Fourth of July came with another disappointing day of holiday expectations. Instead, birthdays were celebrated with spankings, sometimes with the back of large, strong hand and sometimes with a long, black, leather belt. While other children opened presents Christmas morning and celebrated a jolly fat man climbing down their chimney, I endured hours of pain, reflected by the cigarette burns on the nape of my neck. The Fourth of July fireworks in my house was made up of being tied to a chair, forced to watch any toys I did have being blown to bits with M-80's and packs of Black Cats.

Yes, it was then as the bits of flesh spun round and round, painting the beige sink red like a frantic paintbrush, that I realized that I had become numb to what I had been doing and in fact, there are just two people who earned the right to be next on the list. An elite list, that once these two-people joined, I could finally be free.

Yes, mom and dad, I mean you. I know, I know. To you it sounds like I have been rambling on and on. Me free and wandering this room and waving my large knife in the air. You both, gagged and tied down to the dining room table. It was important, to me, that you heard my story. You didn't raise a son who one day would become a doctor, saving lives late at night in the ER. You didn't raise a son with a wall of degrees and palaces around the world. In fact, you didn't raise a son at all. To raise a son requires love and nurturing. You raised a monster, feeding off your years of torture and pain.

The tables have turned on you finally, mom and dad, literally, as you are tied down to this table. My years of field experience together with years of pain brought on both of you brought me here, brought us here. Whatever you did today, you did for the last time. When you went to the grocery store, did you realize that it would be for the last time? But who, you moan under the gag of Pine Soll-soaked rags in your mouth, goes first. Should it be the man who, instead of teaching me how to play catch or drive a car, bonded with his son through regular beatings. Or should it be you mom, who instead of attending school music concerts or providing soup when I was sick, basked in watching me cry with a whack with your wooden spoon.

No, wriggling won't help you father. You look like a marlin flopping around, begging for the warm embrace of the ocean. And no mother, your tears will not loosen the rope across your neck. Soon, soon it will all be over. You both will be dead and I will disappear, start a new life. No one will ever know it was me, never know it was because of you and no one will ever know where I went. I know who I was, who I am, a man who takes lives for the sport, for the revenge against you, because of the pain you caused me. Serial am I.

I have special plans for you father so just hang tight.

Now, don't try to scream out too loud mother as I slide this knife deep into your sternum toward your cold, black heart.

I may be a killer but after-all, I am a gentleman and as always, ladies first.

IF THESE WALLS COULD TALK

I am the creak on the stairs, the cold breeze on the back of your ankle and the witness to lives that are not mine. I am not here to harm you. As a matter of fact, I am not sure why I am still here; trapped within the horse hair, plaster and lathe that has been my prison for over a century.

My eternal clothes look nothing like yours. I am a silent witness to the world that keeps spinning, a shell of the person I once was, soulless.

I don't remember what it means to feel my own pain, love or happiness. But I do feel the heat of your hate when you argue over finances; I feel the warmth of your passion when you caress each other in bed; I feel the coolness when you are ill and I feel the chill when another one of you cease to exist and join me in my prison.

You don't see me. I don't want you to. But you know that I am there. The light in the room that you didn't turn on. The chilling feeling of not being alone in the basement. Your dog stirs and stares at something beyond your sight for no reason. The faint orb protecting your sleeping baby in his crib.

I am not alone. A century of souls share your home, my home. Each with a story of how they got here yet with no memory of it. How did I get here? Why am I not where I was told I would go- heaven? Is it not real? Hell? Is this it? Or, are we somewhere in between? Trapped and intertwined in your life, observing everything, knowing everything.

On an endless loop, day after day and year after year, I watch you sleep, gripping your blanket and holding it close to your chin. Is this for warmth or protection? I watch as you eat, over-indulging in foods that never seem to fill your appetite. I see you everywhere. In the yard where I cannot go, the third floor where the darkest of us all waits, just waits. No space is off limits to my eternal surveillance. Even in the bathroom, privacy is not an option in a house cramped with lost souls.

When you say good night and close your bedroom door, you are not alone. When you walk into the darkened hallway, I am there. Turning on the light may comfort you but know that I am still there. Where else would I go? Where else can I go?

Over a century of living has filled this house, my house. and I can only observe as my world slowly disappears around me. First, the rose-petal wallpaper is peeled off in haste and the wall painted red. Did you know that my grandmother gave me that wallpaper as a wedding gift on my 1st anniversary? Do you care? Yes, I was married but where is he? How did he get beyond these walls?

I move freely here but my earthly body remains trapped within the walls, rotting and decomposing just beyond your Frigidaire. That dress, once white with bright daisies, now grey, covered in dust and plaster. My skin has rotted away or has been eaten by the squirrels and mice that live within your walls. They use my body as their nest. My chest that once contained a heart that loved, is now filled with broken wood and stolen scraps. A home to these dirty creatures. There is nothing I can do but watch my own decay.

The mice are unafraid of us. Scurrying through our soulless bodies. Would you run out of the house, my house, screaming if you knew where my body was? If you only

knew just how close you sat by my rotting shell every day.
From floor to ceiling and from the basement to the attic, our
bodies are everywhere. Entrapped in this tomb you call
home. You cleaned the "dust" from the concrete floor in
the basement. But, the ashes from the lost little boy gone
missing years ago still encrust those stone walls. His sister's
bones lay buried under the rose garden in the backyard. For
years, their father searched for his lost children, only to
abandon this home with his wife, a mother who escaped this
place but left behind a tragic secret.

The children still play here. Laughing in the halls during the
day and crying at night, searching for their father and
cowering in fear at the thought of seeing their mother. Can
you hear them? Can you hear their cries, their laughter? Or
is the sound coming from the speakers in your flat screen
television too loud? No sound can drown out the pain.

Do you hear the screams next to the fireplace when you
hang the garland across the mantel at Christmas? No, you
sing carols and play holiday music. The poor mason, stilled
trapped under a ghostly pile of bricks just at your feet. The
original fireplace collapsed and killed one of the workmen.
Did you know that? Can you feel the death that surrounds

your happy home? The pumpkin and spice candle fills the room and comforts you. The scent is not strong enough to mask our sorrow.

You gather on the couch and hold your children close as you watch Christmas cartoons; not realizing how close I am. How close my body is to yours. Entrapped in the wall behind you. Right behind you. Touch the wall. Can you feel me just on the other side?

The ghostly siblings play in the toy room with your son's toys; sometimes breaking a leg off an action figure or hiding a Lego in the easy chair cushion. The brother, restless, watches your children play on their electronic devices. He has learned how to play those electronic games when the device is left on the kitchen counter, unattended. His favorite game- erase. Erase the games from the screen.

His sister likes to brush her hair, over and over again on an endless loop. Your hairbrush is her favorite. Nothing here belongs to only you. It is ours. What else do we have?

You clean and clean the house but the pain we feel is never washed away. As you sweep the living room floor near the fireplace, the mason reaches out to you for help, eternally trapped, crushed. He reaches for your ankles when you walk by with the broom. If you saw him would you help him? Would you help any of us?

Soon, your time will come and you will join us. One of you will not leave this house. This is what happens. The siblings cannot leave. The mason. Me. Trapped forever and left behind by anyone who knew us. The same will happen to one of you, whether by tragedy or planning, one of your bodies will remain. The mice entangle themselves between the plaster and lathe and wait for a fresh feast. Stolen bits of food and gnawing on my rotted bones are no longer satisfying for them.

One, maybe two, or perhaps all of you will stay, forever. Then you will understand. Finally, you will learn that you were never alone. A new family will move in. They will paint over your red walls and your history will be erased with one stroke of a brush. Erased, just like you did to me.

Fading away like the once bright white daisies on my dress, any trace of you will go. No one will remember you or care. Never existing. Like a ghost.

A DAY IN THE SUN

The Florida sun was especially bright that day. The humidity was so intense, it felt like we were walking through water. But that didn't matter because we were in the happiest place on earth and it was your first time there. It was going to be an incredibly magical day.

You were six years old then, Max. Your world consisted of Spider-Man, Spider-Man and more Spider-Man. You wore Spider-Man sneakers, blue shorts and a red shirt with black webs all over it. Your digital Spidey watch was secured to your wrist and you were prepared to battle the day with your sunglasses on in the shape of Spider-Man's eyes. My little super hero, ready to conquer the kingdom.

The boat met us and the other visitors at the dock of our resort. I remember the look on your face when we cleared the tall pine trees and you had your first view of the castle. You were so excited and you gave me the biggest hug. I can still feel your tiny arms around my neck.

First off the boat, we dashed our way to the entry gates and made our way through the train tunnel. Out on the other side, we entered another world filled with music, the smell of freshly popped popcorn, and gooey chocolate chip cookies. I had a map but you seemed to know exactly where you were headed. Your gram, grandad, father and I could hardly keep up! I knew then that it wasn't a good idea to break in new shoes and boy did I pay for it later.

We made our way down the main street, edging closer to the castle, weaving in and out of strollers and workers holding handfuls of red, blue, green and pink balloons, so many in fact, you asked if they were going to lift the people high into the sky.

We stopped in front of the castle for a family photo. We were already drenched in sweat, regardless that it was only nine o'clock in the morning. That's central Florida for you.

After a quick announcement and a blast of fireworks in the air, the crowd rushed off into different directions like spokes reaching out toward the edges of a bicycle tire. We made our way through the castle and you were so excited to see the drawbridge. The inside hallway of the castle was lined with mosaic tiles that displayed a story of a fairytale princess. Back out into the sun, you found yourself face to face with a carousel, spinning with the most beautiful horses you had ever seen.

The Spider-Man watch beeped and Max looked down toward his wrist, taking his eyes briefly off the fantasy world around him.

We rode the carousel and then it was time for your first roller coaster. The attraction was really built for little children in mind so it didn't have loops or big drops or anything. Your father called it a beginner coaster, and he couldn't wait for you to get older to take you on the big roller coasters at Magic Falls.

Max's mom wiped her cheeks.

The breeze on the ride felt really nice. The turns were easy but at a good pace, not too fast and we loved how it had the seven little dwarves singing their song in the middle of it.

From there, we blasted off to the future and you got to ride on a race car track with your grandad. We knew you would be in good hands with him. For one, he never drove fast and two, your car was on a track. You couldn't go anywhere but forward. Worst case, you'd just bump the car in front of you. We got a great picture of the two of you in your red race car. You said it looked like Spider-Man's car. Your grandad loved you so much and he had that picture of the two of you on his nightstand.

From the racetrack, it was off to battle aliens and an evil emperor on a fun arcade shooting ride and after a pit stop and buying our first of many bottles of water for the day, we got in line to get an autograph from your favorite space ranger. You were to the moon and beyond when you got to meet the ranger, second only to the web slinger. He gave you a high five and together you called his command center in search of bad guys. Another photo and then gram had to get off her feet. We boarded a train that circled the park and got off after two stops.

Many of the rides in the Wild West section of the park were too big for you but we were able to catch a breather from the Florida air by watching a show sung by robotic bears. We clapped along to the finale and you giggled the loudest in the room when the little raccoon popped out of the grey bear's hat. We waved goodbye to the moose, buffalo and deer heads that sung us out of the show and we headed toward what looked like old time colonial America.

We got in line to visit a beautiful mansion and luckily, you weren't afraid of the dark yet. The mansion was a ghost ride but just for fun. Regardless of how many ghosts were in that house, we were just looking forward to another enclosed attraction with air conditioning. We had to wait quite a few minutes to get in but at least the green awning covered everyone and kept us out of the direct sun.

Max heard the beeping again and looked down toward his watch.

The ride was fun but one time was enough for you we thought. Before heading to lunch, it was our time to fly over the streets of London following a magical fairy and children on their way to a land where they never grow up. We took so many pictures in that ride. You wanted to go again and again but it had one of the longest lines in the whole park and we said we would try again after lunch. Max's mom wiped her cheek again. We never did get to go back on that ride that day. The line just grew longer and longer. How people will stand in line for anything for seventy-five minutes is beyond me.

We did so many other fun rides that day. We cruised through a jungle and survived a giant plastic snake, snuck past a hungry family of lions and even saw both sides of a waterfall. We went on another boat ride with pirates, flew on magic carpets, sat back and listened to singing tropical birds and even saw a 3-D show with some of your other favorite characters.

The afternoon parade was fun and the performers and characters on the floats waved to you.

We then went back to our resort and your grandparents took a nap while we swam in the big pool. The water felt so nice and you even went on the pool slide a few times by yourself.

After the sun went down, we went back into the park and got up close to the castle. It was so beautiful all lit up. It even sparkled. We watched a parade with lights and then the finale of the night was a huge firework display above the castle. It was the biggest fireworks show you had ever seen. There were a few loud booms that you didn't care for. You covered your ears a few times but the songs that went along with the display were all your favorites.

The beeping from his wrist sounded again and distracted Max from the show that illuminated the night sky above with hues of green, blue and purple.

The park closed and like cattle being rushed off the pasture, everyone pushed and shoved their way to the exit. Tired of getting our heels nipped by strollers, we slipped into a big store on a corner and we bought you a big stuffed animal. Well, it wasn't an animal really but a stuffed and soft version of your favorite space ranger. The moment you saw the row of them, conveniently on the second shelf perfect for six year olds I might add, you grabbed one and wouldn't let go. We either had to buy it for you or let the shopkeeper stick a price tag on your bottom. There was no separating the two of you.

Back at the hotel, you introduced your new friend to your stuffed Spider-Man and the three of you fell asleep in no time flat, Spider-Man under one arm and the ranger under the other. What a great picture. We could not have asked for a more amazing day. I would give anything to have just one more day like that.

Max's mom folded the scrapbook on her lap closed and tossed a tissue in the waste basket next to her chair. She reached her arm out and held onto her son's hand. His Spider-Man and space ranger stuffed friends were tucked under the blanket next to him and the machines beside his bed beeped as they monitored his vitals and kept his small body alive. He had been in a coma ever since the accident.

Max's family had said their goodbyes and his mom wanted to tell him one last story before she had to say goodbye to her son for the last time.

She leaned in, kissed his forehead and whispered, 'I love you'. Tears raced down her cheeks as the doctors turned off the machines and the beeping stopped.

GALACTIC CASUALTIES OF WAR

Thornton Wallace III descended from a long line of well-to-do and well-respected community figures. His grandfather was the Grand Master to oversee the Masonic jurisdiction in the northeast while his father was aspiring to be Worshipful Master of the lodge in their hometown of Scottsfield. Both his grandfather and father have left their mark on the community in more ways than one. The elementary school was named after his grandfather and his father just donated a hefty sum of cash to expand the hospital. Once construction was complete, the new cancer research wing will be named after him and Thornton's mother. She lost her battle with cancer three years ago, and Thornton's father did what he knew best by diving into his work and giving back to the community even more, all to make a name for himself.

Thornton was as motivated as his grandfather and father but not in the ways of adding value to the community or being a leader to freemasons. He would rather strive to be commander of Squadron 45, the most gifted and talented Stealth Elf or even, the most powerful wizard in all of Razmos. Thornton's glory and fame came to him when the power light flashed blue on one of his video game consoles.

In the online gaming world, Thornton was a leader, a hero, a god. In the real world, well, not so much. He lived in realms beyond earth, battled alien commandos on Mars, scavenged for supplies and firearms on alien sub-cruisers at the bottom of the Pacific and even saved a Viking princess from the clutches of the evil three-headed troll dragon. However, in reality, his realm was not as adventurous or exciting. His empire was the four walls of the basement in his father's home.

The faded-green couch clung to his backside like an outfielder's hand in a well-worn baseball glove. The right arm of the couch was stained with nacho-cheese dusted claw marks and the coffee table was littered with crinkled wrappers from local various fast-food entities. Yellow and blue wrappers piled high on each other with crusted cheese bits and ketchup stains while aged blackened guacamole clung to foil wrappers. A six-pack of neon green soda sat huddled close to each other, still bound by the linking plastic rings. Four of the bottles were empty and a fifth was half-empty, the carbonation escaping three days ago, leaving a sugar-filled flat liquid that he would eventually drink anyway.

Thornton had everything he needed in the basement and never had to leave, rarely getting up from the sofa except to use the bathroom or grab his next meal, left on the stairs. The housekeeper kept him feed, three times a day with his favorite fast-food meals. Sometimes Thornton would get motivated and swap out a bag of wrappers and cardboard containers for a fresh meal but usually the garbage piled up around him for weeks at a time before the housekeeper felt brave and cleaned up the mess.

Thornton landed the ideal job for himself, video game tester at Epic III Studios and he was by far, their best tester. It was up to him to find any programming mistakes, glitches and figure out the cheat codes. If he could defeat the games too easily, the game went back to the drawing board or headed onto store shelves at reduced price. Epic III Studios heavily relied on him and more than he realized, Thornton relied on them. In the real world, Thornton didn't have any friends and the closest he came to a relationship with a girl was while playing *War Cry IV*. One of his online companions was Queen Destiny 38 and they blasted their way through levels together for a few days until they reached the main reactor on the rebel's base. While having her back turned, he fired a proton cannon and she was out. She would have to wait two hours before respawning, giving him plenty of time to take out the reactor to become the sole champion.

Ever since his high-school graduation and stumbling across the game tester ad in a Power Games magazine, Thornton was glued to his television and game console. Video games were presented to him on a regular basis, first by mail and, more often than not, sent digitally to one of his gaming systems.

Galactic Casualties of War was one of his favorite games of all time. He loved its special effects and the feeling of being immersed in an alien world, commander of Green Squadron and fighting alien lizard- bat hybrid soldiers. It took him a week to get to the final level, freezing the core of the alien planet and then blowing it out of the Nebulous Solar System. In the final moments of the game credits, he saw a glimmer of an alien ship disappear into deep space, an obvious signal to a game sequel.

He found racing games boring. Upgrading vehicles and swapping out tires, adding detail work and being chased around a city by police or round and round on a world-class circuit track did nothing for him. To Thornton, there was no imagination or skill required. Epic III Studios may have well sent him games of dogs chasing their tales over and over again.

And two-dimensional games with cute characters wearing overalls or bouncing around like pink blobs of goo were the absolute worst. It was not believable that by changing a character's overalls from blue to white somehow gave the silly man the ability to shoot fireballs out of his fingertips. Where did the large villain turtle come from and why would he keep kidnapping the same princess? Wouldn't his land of oversized beasts and turtles with spiked-armored shells be more exciting than a world where the character repeatedly jumped over potted Venus Fly Traps and found it difficult to avoid chubby moles? No, not his speed at all. He played the game, beat the main villain as always, and emailed the bosses at Epic III Studios with his feedback. His feedback, often a few short words like fun, worth playing, same old same old or his favorite word, "awesome".

Thornton set his game controller down beside him and reached for a handful of cheese balls in the large clear plastic tub beside him, his most faithful sidekick. He shoved six cheese balls into his mouth and grabbed the controller again and continued to play *World of Avalon*. Tiny bits of orange wedged themselves into the crevasses around the green circle and red triangle button on the controller.

"The End". He had done it again, another game completed and another world saved by magical owl beasts wearing glasses. He shook his head in disdain and wondered how anyone would believe that if the magical owls had the brain capacity to invade a world with space ships and sonic blasters, how in all cheese balls could they not correct their vision. "Totally unbelievable," he said to himself.

Once the game credits finished, the screen flashed white and a keyboard appeared. Using the arrows on his controller, he selected letters on the keyboard and spelled out "same old same old" and then selected submit.

He exhaled in frustration and grabbed one of the neon green sodas and drank the entire thing.

A message appeared on his screen that read, "*Galactic Casualties of War* II download in progress". He belched in excitement and the download bar on the screen could not move fast enough. He had waited two years for this moment, wasted time battling turtles, leaped over canyons in futuristic Camaros and ate power pellets in Pac Man Remix after Pac Man Remix.

He took a deep breath and could feel himself becoming Commander of Green Squad again. The download bar read 45 percent and in a manner of minutes, he would be back in deep space, battling those aliens who got away in the original *Galactic Casualties of War*.

Another message appeared on the screen that read, "Please Connect Virtual Scanner and Headset now. Cannot locate virtual controls."

In an instant, things went from awesome to out of this world freakin' amazing. He knew virtual reality games were coming but had no idea they already arrived and, best of all, released for *Galactic Casualties of War II*.

The housekeeper opened the basement door and yelled down to him, "Thornton, a box arrived for you. I also have your dinner. Come and get them." She placed the box and bag of tacos on the top step and closed the door. Thornton boosted himself from the sofa, pushing off the sofa's arm for momentum and support. He felt a little light headed and dizzy, thinking he either got up too quickly, the neon green soda went right to his head or he was overcome with excitement at seeing the contents of the box. He climbed a few stairs until he was close enough to grab the box and bag of tacos. He tossed the bag on the sofa cushion and packets of medium and hot sauce spilled out onto the floor.

He used the box to push aside the wrappers on the coffee table and ripped it open quickly like a kid on Christmas morning. It was exactly what he had been waiting his entire life for- the crisp new box inside with a picture of a virtual headset and controllers. The child on the box cover looked like he was having the time of his life.

Thornton shredded the boxes and lifted the headset into the air, holding it high into the recessed lighting like Indiana Jones victoriously holding a golden idol. He carefully set it down on the arm of the sofa.

Bits of white styrofoam floated into the air and clung to his hairy knuckles as he pulled the Virtual Scanner out from its box. He connected it to the game console and dug deeper into the large box until he removed two new controllers, electric blue with silver lightning bolts painted on each side.

The download bar on the screen read 90 percent and the message on the screen changed to "Virtual Scanner Located. Virtual Headset located."

He slid his thumbs over the controllers in each of his hands and a red light flashed in the corner of each controller. "Game, set, match," he smiled.

He plopped back down on the sofa and the bag of tacos were smooshed between his left butt cheek and the cushion. He lifted his rear end up just enough to slide the bag to the side and another hot sauce packet fell to the floor.

The download bar read 100 percent and then the words "Place Virtual Headset on now" flashed on the screen.

Not willing to let go of his new powerful controllers, he grabbed the Virtual Headset and slid the black band around his head and over his ears. The wide dark glasses covered most of his face.

"Totally awesome," he said.

A futuristic symphonic sound blasted from the speakers and as the words *Galactic Casualties of War II: Return of the Kryvons* appeared, the controllers vibrated in his hands. "Way awesome," he said.

He sat patiently, like a dog begging for a treat, while he watched the intro video. He learned his prized Green Squadron had been wiped out during an ambush of Kryvons and he was the last original solider reaming. Left nearly for dead, he was revived by nearby freedom fighters. They had to come to terms with their interplanetary differences to defeat the hoard of Kryvons before the seven moons became aligned. Once aligned, the moons would give the Kryvons the ability to open a portal to other realms and their insatiable need to feast on other worlds would become unstoppable. "It's totally up to me," Thornton said. "This is what I have been training for. Let's do this."

As the opening story wrapped up, Thornton reached down and rubbed his leg, suddenly stiff and throbbing. He was about to remove his Virtual Headset to check it out when the first battle sequence began and he found himself surrounded by a hoard.

Level after level, Thornton felt more and more like he was actually in the game, in the world of Kryvons, the freedom fighters, and interplanetary market places.

By level three, he had gained enough silver bits to upgrade his ship. By level four, the cause of his leg pain moved from the vein in his leg and passed through his right femoral vein.

By level five, he was blasting Kryvon spaceships into bits of moon dust and the tiny clot found its way to his right external iliac and then his common iliac.

During a brief moment of hibernation, Thornton put down the controllers and reached for the bag of tacos, now cold after hours of game play. He unwrapped one of the tacos and shoved it quickly into his mouth. The top of the shell remained hard but the bottom was soggy from the grease of seasoned hamburger meat and sour cream.

Unexpectedly, a Kryvon appeared on his ship and tried to break the glass of his hibernation chamber. Thornton quickly grabbed his controllers and he had to find the release button to wake his character up or die.

After a quick battle and ejecting an escape pod out of his ship just in time, he was on his way to the freedom fighter's base on the Hemora Sea Planet. He didn't know that the clot also boosted itself into his inferior vena cava toward his right atrium.

"Years in the making," Thornton said to the screen as his pod neared the base. Little did he know how his words rang true, but no only to his glory of returning to the world of *Galactic Casualties of War*, but about the clot that had formed in his leg. From years of sitting, eating fast food and drinking sugary carbonated beverages that could burn the paint off cars, his sedentary lifestyle had come with a price.

His escape pod landed at the Hemora Sea Planet base and he joined the freedom fighters for an epic battle. Using his bounty of silver bits, he loaded himself up with level ten firearms and armor. He felt invincible and nothing could harm him.

Unfortunately, deep beneath his armor and layers of protection, the clot reached his right atrium, passed to the right ventricle and eventually found its way to his lung, circulating though the pulmonary artery and its branches.

The base doors slid open and Thornton rose to his feet and prepared himself for war. As he had gotten the first glimpse of the size of the Kryvon's epic army, an excruciating pain radiated from his chest and he immediately felt light-headed. He shook his head back and forth, thinking that wearing the Virtual Headset for so long had taken its toll on his eyes. His heart raced faster and faster and he began to cough. His cough continued and soon his cough became wet. Because he failed to remove the Virtual Headset, Thornton didn't realize that he was coughing up blood. With each wet cough, he wiped his hands across his shirt, the dark blood smearing against the bits of nacho cheese dust and sour cream on his chest.

Laser fire and sonic blasts rocked the screen and the controllers in his hands vibrated violently. His hands gripped his controllers in a quick, sudden burst and he fell back onto the sofa. The taco bag slid off the sofa and the wrapped tacos poured onto the floor. Like a fish flopping on the deck of a SeaRay, Thornton's body seized and froze. His eyes bulged and the last thing he saw as the Pulmonary Embolism ceased his life was a Kryvon soldier standing over him and a beam from its sonic blaster rocketing toward his face.

CAROL OF THE BELLS

Henry drove down the tree-lined back highway, on his way home like he did every night. The snow clouds blocked out any of the night sky above and the light flurries that slid off his windshield on the interstate now started to come down a little thicker and began to stick to the glass. Listening to a holiday radio station to put him a good mood after a long day at work, his favorite Christmas song was just coming on.

> *Hark! How the bells, sweet silver bells*
> *All seem to say, "Throw cares away."*

Henry turned the volume dial up and flipped the lever under his steering wheel. The windshield wipers slowly began to sway against the glass, pushing the snowflakes out of his view.

> *Christmas is here, bringing good cheer*
> *To young and old, meek and the bold*
> *Ding, dong, ding, dong, that is their song,*

His fingertips danced on the steering wheel as he sang along to the radio. The snow fell even harder and began to stick to the branches of the surrounding pine forest.

> *With joyful ring, all caroling*
> *One seems to hear words of good cheer*
> *From everywhere, filling the air*
> *Oh how they pound, raising the sound*
> *O'er hill and dale, telling their tale*

A grey fog hugged the highway and break lights from the cars a few feet ahead of him flashed their red tail lights, slowing down to deal with the weather. The silver Buick in front of him moved over to the right lane. Henry sped up and passed the car and driver, his favorite song motivating him and putting him in a happy holiday mood.

> *On, on they send, on without end*
> *Their joyful tone to every home*
> *Hark! How the bells, sweet silver bells*
> *All seem to say, "Throw cares away."*

The traffic thinned out as more and more commuters found their exits. 10 more miles to go. The snow came down harder and began to cover the road. The weather report called for evening snow showers but not until much later. The front obviously moved in much sooner than he expected. Henry was beginning to rethink that staying a bit later for a last-minute meeting was not such a good idea. He could have taken the conference call on his mobile phone while driving home on time but he hated doing work in the car. He suffered from a bit of road rage and didn't want to call out his favorite profanities while talking to his best customer.

Christmas is here, bringing good cheer
To young and old, meek and the bold
Ding, dong, ding, dong, that is their song

The car slid a little and Henry felt the car give way a bit under his heavy foot. He looked down as his heart sank for a quick moment and realized the speedometer at 80mph. 55mph was the speed limit and with the snow falling even harder, he pressed on the break peddle a little to slow his car down. He then turned the knob a half turn to control his wipers and they sped up, now sprinting back and forth against the glass. The snow was wet and heavy and had begun to gather in the upper corners of the windshield where the wiper blades couldn't reach. He looked in his rearview mirror but he couldn't see out as the snow blanketed the back window. He couldn't believe how quickly the snow picked up. Henry turned on the rear window defroster and soon could see only darkness behind him as the snow melted and slid off the glass. No headlights behind and no red brake lights in front of him. He still sang the words to his favorite song but held the steering wheel a bit tighter, no longer tapping his fingers to the melody.

With joyful ring, all caroling.
One seems to hear words of good cheer
From everywhere, filling the air
O, how they pound, raising the sound
O'er hill and dale, telling their tale

The cell phone nestled in the center console lit up and Henry grabbed it. A text from his wife- *Almost home? Leaving the pet store now. See you soon.* He pressed the top button on his phone to turn off the light on his screen and placed the phone back into the cup holder. There was no way he could send her a text message now. He had to concentrate on the road. Just a mile or two more and he would be at his exit, almost home. The snow was really falling now, heavy and thick, overtaking the sides of the highway. Henry found himself driving in the middle of the two-lane highway, the reflection of the yellow lines against his headlights acted as his guide. He flipped the wipers up as high as they could go and they raced against the glass, chasing each other and doing their best to keep up with the snow. He passed a large green road sign but couldn't see into the fog and snow to read it. He knew he was close and the overpass had to be coming up soon.

Gaily they ring, while people sing
Songs of good cheer, Christmas is here!
Merry, merry, merry, merry, merry Christmas!
Merry, merry, merry, merry, merry Christmas!

The overpass was finally in sight and he could see the orange glow from the familiar street lamp. He slowed down a bit more and turned his right blinker on. Henry looked in the rearview mirror and still did not see any lights. He slid his car fully in the right lane, slipping and sliding in the snow. A brief reprieve from the snow, he drove under the overpass and followed the curved road up the ramp, a 180 degree stretch of road, fully engulfed in snow. He wondered where the snow plows were all at. Not one in sight. Not one spreading salt anywhere to help drivers stay on the road.

No flashing yellow lights from their trucks. The storm obviously took them by surprise too. The plows will be out soon but already behind the eight ball.

The snow fell hard and the wipers on Henry's car could barely keep up. Merging onto the main road from the off-ramp, Henry drove right through the yield sign but luckily for him, there were no cars in the lane. Up ahead, he could see the glow of red lights piercing through the blizzard. A stoplight. He pressed his foot against the break peddle and his car slid on the ice and snow. Henry gripped the wheel and his heart raced while he tried to gain control of his vehicle. Suddenly, two red tail lights lit up the fog and the wipers cleared enough snow from the windshield for henry to see what was just in front him. A tractor-trailer carrying a wide load of steel construction beams had stopped at the traffic light. One of beams smashed through the car's windshield as the front of Henry's car slid under the load and crashed into the back of the truck. The beam continued through the glass and in an instant, ripped through Henry's face, crushing his nose and forcing it and the rest of his skull against the leather headrest. The foam from the headrest exploded with bits of Henry, spraying the backseat with human and Detroit shrapnel. The airbag launched out of the steering wheel and compressed against his headless body, still strapped into the seat. Henry's fingers slowly slid off the wheel. His favorite song still rang out from the radio.

On, on they send, on without end
Their joyful tone to every home.

Emergency vehicles quickly took over the scene and any passing traffic, few and far between in the storm, were forced to one lane. A white minivan approached and slowed as it passed the carnage. The driver quickly glancing toward the passenger window but unable to see all that happened or who it happened to. As she drove away, the flashing lights from the ambulance reflected on the large yellow bag of dog food in the backseat.

Ding dong ding dong...
Dumm...

BARRY LAKE

Barry Lake was a staple aboard the Heaven on the Seas. He reclined back in his lounge chair by the pool on the Lido deck. His brown freckles appeared painted on his tanned and leather sun-dried skin. The longer he soaked up the sun, the more his tiny island of brown pigmentations merged into continents.

An avid adventurer ever since his navy days in Honolulu, Barry enjoyed seeing the world and all of the wonders it held. More of a sea man than a sky guy, Barry preferred to travel via water vessel than a metal tube with wings that, to him, miraculously maintained altitude and not fall out of the sky. He had been on two flights his entire life- one to the navy base and one back to the mainland when his tour of duty had completed.

In his early twenties, Barry tried to enjoy civilian life on dry land but the sea always called to him. A few years later, after dodging the marriage bullet to a woman who ended up being the harlot of the Globe Trailer Park of eastern Idaho, he inherited a large sum of money from his parents when they passed away suddenly after losing a dog fight with a speeding train. Take note kids, when the railroad crossing gates come down, it doesn't mean that one more car can squeeze through. The CSX operated engine turned the wood-paneled station wagon into a twisted mess of metal and dazzling fireworks as it pushed the inhabited vehicle down the tracks. The remains of Barry's parents twisted and shredded in the wreck were a mess but fortunately for him, their will was squeaky clean.

Never having to lift a finger for himself or punch the average-Joe time clock day in and day out, Barry set out to explore the world, via cruise ship of course. The captain, pilot, navigator and all important bar-host, took him on many Sex-on-the-Beach adventures from cruising across the Atlantic Ocean to visit ports in Istanbul, Rome, Florence and Sicily to navigating their way to the northern shores of Norway and the Arctic Circle. Wherever the ship went, Barry went. Money truly made the world go round and Barry found himself a permanent home on the Verandah deck.

His spacious suite included a large deck, big enough for a table and chairs to accommodate dinner for six, a living room area with a large flat-screen television, couch, and wet bar. The bedroom contained a large king-sized bed with an unobstructed view of the water and the en suite master bathroom included a garden tub, shower and double vanity sink, almost twice the size of the second bathroom just off the living room. The cabin number on the door, 7614, was replaced with a plaque that read "Lake Residence". With daily housekeeping and evening turn-down service including two chocolates on his pillow, Barry truly led a life of luxury. Cleaning latrines in the tropical heat and taking orders from an overly-assertive sergeant who obviously compensated for a large forehead and tiny penis, Barry was light years away from anywhere he or anyone else thought he would ever be. So long Angie, the mobile home hussy of the Wild West, this man was set to live the high life.

Even though it was nearly impossible for his fortune to run out, Barry was a recluse, only speaking to the captain and few members of the crew. His best friend, if you could call her that, was a bar server named Chloe who knew when and how to serve him his daily dose of vodka. A Bloody Mary, extra ice and extra bloody with a freshly-washed celery stalk and kabob of chilled shrimp at 9am. This was followed later by a Chocolate Monkey- vodka, chocolate, banana and fresh mint blended smooth with ice in a tall glass at 2pm and then a vodka with an olive on the rocks before and after his evening meal. Barry quickly learned that too much liquor on any given day was not a good thing, especially when his days were spent soaking in the sun in the northern or southern hemispheres. Chloe ensured that he had plenty of fluids. With every cocktail came a large glass of water- extra ice.

Now, soaking in the mid-afternoon rays of the sun, Barry lay on his favorite lounge chair, sunglasses on and head back against the blue and white striped towel. The book he had been reading, *The Old Man and the Sea*, a favorite of his ever since he once met Ernest Hemingway in a bar in Idaho, had dropped to his lap. His fingers tangled in the pages as though too exhausted to bear the weight of the book any longer. The sea breeze rolled in from deck 9 above and it gently and playfully danced throughout his thin, wispy white hair.

Heaven on the Seas set sail four days ago for a 22-day voyage around South America, scheduled to stop in various ports in Brazil, Argentina, Peru, and Columbia with a mid-stop on the northernmost tip of Antarctica- a trip Barry had taken over and over this season. He had been looking forward to this voyage as it was the last of the season. Soon, the ship would set sail for a new destination around Indonesia. He was energized with the opportunity to see a new place and even more energized that this particular set of cruise guests would not be on his next one. Typically, a ship that attracted senior citizens to it just as much as the early-bird buffet at China Kingdom or Southern Jones' BBQ All-You-Can-Eat, the crowd this go round was filled with families- mothers, fathers and worst of all, small children.

Unfortunately for Barry, these children weren't the ones raised in military school or far away upscale boarding schools where manners were just as important as grades. No, these children, raised by hand-held electronics and absent parents, were untamed tiny creates with an insatiable appetite for cannon bombs in the pool and french fries, ketchup, french fries and even more ketchup, only to be outdone by the bowlful mounds of chocolate and vanilla ice cream that was left to melt away in the tropical sun. Indoor voices a thing of the past and apparently ignored during the last bit of summer vacation, the high-pitch squeal of little girls rattled Barry's ears as intensely as a whistle training a dog.

The lengthy list of hot tub rules were ignored by the toddlers and elementary-aged kids splashing about like lobsters boiling in a pot on the stove. Amongst the waves, a sea of tiny arms strangled by inflated images of cartoon fish and beloved animated characters.

Barry lay back on his lounge chair, out cold and zoned out from the rest of the world moving and shaking around him, despite the constant chatter, disarray of deck games from ping pong to corn hole to screams of "cannon ball" and "no (small child's name inserted here) don't splash me, I'm telling mommy!", Barry seemed to be in a world of his own.

Like a mother hawk circling her prey, Chloe honed in on Barry and set a fresh Chocolate Monkey and glass of iced water on the side table next to him. "Enjoy Mr. Lake," she said as she removed an empty water glass.

Adalai Richards cruised often with her husband Earl and she found herself next to Barry. Only a small round cocktail table separated their chairs but it could have been miles away. Adalai was in deep chatter with her husband about their port excursions, specifically about the service they received, or absence of any sort of service, a topic more of value to her than the excursion itself. I'd say that they were conversing but a conversation between two people requires dialogue between two willing parties and Earl, married to Adalai for forty-five years, smiled in the direction of his wife, eyes closed behind his reflective sunglasses she purchased during the dog days of summer sale at the Beall's department store.

Adalai clamored on about how the air-conditioning in the taxi cab was no match for the heat. What would have helped, of course, is if she had closed the windows but the deodorant choice, or lack thereof, of the driver, forced the couple to endure the heat and humidity, as well as the dirt-filled air as they toured the small village just beyond the port.

As Adalai continued her tirade, the only movement from Barry's chair was the slight flapping of the pages of his book. He hadn't lathered himself in sunblock since eight that morning and the sun was taking its toll on his skin. The sun spots and freckles seemed to appear darker against the contrast of his reddening leather skin. Like tiny islands in a sea of molten lava, Barry was clearly due for another dose of his coconut-scented sun protection, PS 45.

Ranting more and more about the cost of their lunch, Adalai, who failed to notice the burst of gas Barry released into the air thanks to an extra helping of sausage at breakfast, every so often glanced away from her husband, whose snores were drowned out by the happy carefree screams calling out "Marco" and "Polo." Adalai fired warning stares at the plethora of children cannon-bombing their bodies into the pool, splashing everyone from the newlyweds who dipped their toes in at the corner of the pool to the twin boys engrossed in a tug-of-war match over neon green goggles. The boys' parents didn't have the forethought to purchase a second pair from Walgreens prior to boarding and now refused to spend just under ten dollars for a pair from the ship's gift shop. Sunblock and aloe lotion sold for the price of gold onboard and the parents who did pack an ample supply of lotion, lathered their children ferociously. Fogs of lotion clouds filled the air and encrusted the whipped cream from Pina Coladas and Strawberry Daiquiris while gobs of white goo coated tiny bodies like fresh paint on a time-worn wooden fence.

"Be nice to your brother," the twins' mom shouted from her lounge chair, lifting her head out from her romance novel enough to parent her children. Clueless to the ends of oblivion, Shirley called out the general coaching to a pool filled with several sets of brothers. Even if she intended to focus her poor parental instructions toward her children, she seemed to neglect the fact that she had two boys. So which brother was supposed to be nice to the other- a fact that fell on deaf ears to her children? The pointless direction was ignored and the twins continued to pull on the goggles whose fate was not to last a day further on this cruise, let alone another five minutes.

The ship swayed side to side as the Atlantic waves crashed into the port side. Clouds thickened in the distance.

Barry sunk deep into the lounge chair and the patch of white curled hair on his chest twirled in the breeze. Two ice cubes remained in his water glass beside him and held on to their shape the best they could as beads of cool sweat raced down the glass, quickly absorbing into the white cocktail napkin just under the glass.

The intercom blared two loud beeps and the ship's captain spouted on about their current position, wind speed, something about knots in relation to the arrival time at the next port and a thank you for sailing with them. His speech ended with a gentle reminder that crew was available at the reservations desk on deck four for anyone interested in booking their next cruise now to take advantage of steep discounts and the ability to earn a stateroom credit of up to four-hundred dollars.

As the sun slid across the sky, the shadow from Barry's sandals became longer and longer. Almost half past four, the few older couples, including Adalai and Earl who valiantly stayed their ground against the onslaught of endless antics of children, made their way toward the mid-ship elevators to shower and change for the early dinner seating. Adalai continued her rant about the ship's menu options. As a steadfast vegan who also avoided sugar at any cost, her menu options had been limited. She was by far not a happy camper when the afternoon tea just the day before, served finger sandwiches of egg salad, cucumber with cream cheese with a variety of crème puffs, chocolate cakes and fruit tarts with lemon cream.

The main dining room would soon be filled with white pants, tropical shirts, and the whirling sound of motorized mini-scooters as the seniors rushed, like sloths moving through the jungles of Madagascar, to their assigned tables. The wide array of matching couple outfits ranged from Elvis-inspired rhinestone collars with glittery belt buckles to attire that could cause any of the senior crowd to be confused for being Colonel Sanders leading a sermon on a humid Savannah Sunday morning. Fine dining or not, the older crowd would be sure to get their monies worth by ordering several first course and second course items- nibbling at each one and ordering water, iced-tea and lemonade- drinks included in the price of admission. Hard liquor dinks from the well of the bar were to be consumed only during happy hours and bouts of good fortune at the slots and roulette tables. Coffee or tea was the drink of choice during the intense Mahjong tournaments.

The sun had begun to set on the horizon and could be seen through the windows of the Lido deck. It no longer shined down from above but now seemed like a beacon from a distant lighthouse.

Barry remained still in his lounge chair as more and more guests exited the pool area. Shelby called out to her twins again as she wanted them out of the pool to change for dinner. Pruned like a pack of yogurt-covered raisins, the red-headed twins raced from the water. One eye lens from a pair of green goggles lay on the deck while the rest of the pair lay at the bottom of the pool.

One of the twins sat down on a chair beside Barry to slip on his sandals. His wet body dripped everywhere and he shook his head back and forth like a dog stuck in the eye wall of a tornado, flicking the water into the air in every direction. Barry didn't move as the brief toddler shower rained down on him. Beads of water soaked into the pages of his book.

Soon, the attire on the Lido deck transformed from bathing suits that did their best to cover up failed diets, sagging effects of parenthood and aging, and even suits that barely covered up body parts that most of the children wouldn't learn about until middle school health class into freshly bathed and showered children, parents and seniors dressed to the nines. On their way to the main dining room, the Lido deck buffet or off to sign their children in at the kid's club on deck 9, the guests had their fill of the day from the overly chlorinated pool water with just a hint of toddler urine that escaped from generic pool diapers purchased at a shopper's megastore.

Barry remained in his lounge chair until he was the last person lying by the pool. The sky had changed from blue, to shades of pink and purple to finally a royal blue as stars began to peak down toward the Heaven.

The doors slid open by the mid-ship elevators and Chloe stepped out, empty tray in hand. She quickly surveyed the deck for any last-minute bar takers after another ordinary day at sea when she eyed Barry still in his chair. By now, he was typically down in his suite, waiting to have dinner on his private patio. She stepped closer to him and noticed the Chocolate Monkey sat untouched on the side table. The mint garnish had slid off the glass and lay wilted, nearly drowning in the sea of chocolate and melted ice. The water glass was also untouched and the cubes of ice had melted.

"Mr. Lake," she called out. He didn't respond. "Mr. Lake. I think you fell asleep and it's almost dinner time," she said as she reached out to tap his shoulder. He didn't move.

Chloe knelt down beside him and placed her tray on an empty chair. She gently nudged his shoulder and his hand dropped out from his book. The book slid off his lap and onto the deck. Chloe grabbed his wrist and instinctively jumped back when she didn't feel a pulse.

She called the captain who alerted the ship's doctor. Barry Lake had passed away earlier in the day, just after lunch the doctor presumed.

Previously that day, children argued and jumped cannon-ball style into the pool, mothers ignored their kids and fathers huddled close around the pool bar to take advantage of Bud-Light specials, Adalai Richards drolled on about a musty, hot cab ride, while Barry Lake lay dead unnoticed on his lounge chair. The guests enjoyed a day as ordinary as the day before, unknowingly sharing their time with a dead man among them.

A wealthy recluse, Barry's body was removed from the ship at the next port without fanfare or notice. The Heaven on the Seas shoved off to continue her next adventure, one passenger less and with one stateroom suite now available at a discounted rate for the duration of the cruise-room 7614, awaiting its next temporary passenger.

HOARD

The loud boom outside rattled the windows of the fourth-floor loft, waking Alice from a deep sleep. She shifted her body and rolled over the tattered couch cushion she used for a mattress. She raised her head and a few small white feathers clung to her hair as they escaped from a large tear in the side of the stained light blue fabric.

Some sort of commotion was happening down on the street but Alice seemed unfazed as she rubbed her eyes and laid her head back onto the cushion. A tower of newspapers and boxes blocked most of the window and any light from the late morning sun. Outside, the world was buzzing with excitement but in her world, it was quiet, surrounded by stacks of newspapers and mounds of trash. Her clothes were strewn around the apartment and dripped off boxes. Filthy pots and pans spilled out of the cupboards and onto the wooden floor planks. Barely visible, the kitchen faucet stretched itself over piles of cups and plates in the sink. Keeping everything clean was not her top priority.

Another boom from below and a scream and Alice knew it was time to wake up. She had hoped for a calm day but there hadn't been a day of peace in years. She lived alone in the loft and her family stopped visiting her, now living in the countryside. Alice sat up as her eyes searched around the room. The frame that once protected a canvas painting of a local café, hung just above piles of laundry and crinkled paper balls. The canvas itself was torn and used to wipe away remnants of her morning constitution. Alice scoured her home for more paper, anything that would suit the necessary purpose.

She slid her hand over a yellow-stained magazine cover and picked it up. She stared at the glamourous woman on the cover, wrapped in fur and long, sparking diamonds. The Eiffel Tower stood tall in the background, illuminated by the city of lights. She loved the cover and savored it for as long as she could. Alice used every other ounce of paper, canvas and piece of clothing to wrap her waste in. She didn't want to use this cover, a final reminder of what the world was like outside. Surrounded by urine and fecal-soaked belongings,

Alice had no other option than to relieve herself on the prized magazine cover. It was that or unwrap one of the crinkled balls of paper to reuse it but she preferred not to unwrap something she used to flush away out of mind and far out of sight.

Positioning herself to kneel, Alice raised herself slightly off the floor and pulled her skirt down just below her knees. She slid the magazine cover under her and gripped onto a box for support. After a few moments of pushing, she felt the release of pressure and the model on the magazine cover was no longer properly dressed for her night on the town.

Alice slid her skirt back up around her and without looking down, she carefully rolled the magazine cover up and tucked it away into one of the boxes under a pair of ragged pantyhose. The loft was a mess yet tossing out any trash was not an option for her.

Next on her list for the morning was to find something to eat. She had not stepped outside the loft in almost a year. Her once bountiful stash of food was almost gone and after mold and mice did away with the fresh produce and bread, she was left with rice, potatoes and now incredibly hard salami. Each day she hoped that her family would come to visit and more importantly, replenish her stock of food. With each passing day, she grew more tired and hungry, rationing what she had. Her body ached so much that often her rodent co-habitants seemed like a good food option. Unfortunately, they moved quickly throughout the piles of her old life that she was not able to catch any of them. Instead, they left tiny trails of black droppings behind. The mice mainly kept to the piles of laundry and waste under the picture-less frame, scavenging on whatever her body had expelled over the past few months.

No matter how chilly the loft had gotten, she knew better than to use the blanket her great grandmother had knitted. Alice crammed the blanket in the corner a few months ago after an agonizing night of nearly being devoured by fleas. The bites on her legs and arms itched for days and the bites on her back were the worst. She had to use the edges of the boxes to relieve herself from the itching and with each pass, stirred the smell of drying feces and urine like a witch mixing a brew of rotted flesh.

Alice had grown accustomed to the smell, her furry companions and clutter closing in around her. Once sickened by the smell of rotting bananas in the market, her nose no longer noticed the stench that wafted into the hallway through the small crack under her front door. A locked bolt and three chains kept her inside and she was just fine with that.

Alice had not had a shower in months, since the water and electricity had been shut off in her building and she hadn't applied an ounce of make-up since the night she ate her last tube of lipstick, pretending it was strawberry ice cream.

She walked to the kitchen table and picked up a brush and cracked hand-mirror. She positioned the mirror just right so a ray of light from outside reflected off the glass and highlighted her silhouette. She gently ran the brush through her hair and its teeth fought their way through knots and forced the clingy feathers out. Alice was unaware of the feathers and continued to brush her hair peacefully as another boom rocked the street below.

Once satisfied that her hair was free of knots and most importantly, any small crawly things that had hoped to find a new place to call home, she placed the brush and mirror back onto the table and looked around the kitchen. Each cabinet door hung open and most of the dishes were piled high on the counter and in the sink. Assuming the luxury of water may vanish, Alice had filled glasses, pitchers, saucers, bowls, pots, and flower vases with water. She filled the clawfoot tub with water as well. Each vessel was stored in the bathroom, surrounding the tub. Evaporation and thirst did away with most of her supply and Alice rationed the precious source of life as much as she could stand. Her stomach cried out for food and her throat ached for water.

Choosing water over substance, Alice grabbed a crystal vase from the kitchen table. She lifted it to her eyes and swirled the remnants of water around. As the rust-colored fluid swirled around the base, bits of black droppings spun around like ants circling a whirlpool. Convincing herself that the tiny rounded black bits were ants, she closed her eyes and took a large gulp, finishing all of the vase's contents. She swallowed hard and rubbed her throat as she placed the vase back onto the table. She still had enough water in the various containers in the bathroom for a few more weeks. Disappointed over her choice of water over substance, Alice's stomach moaned with delight with the surprise of the six little pellets that rushed down her throat with the water.

She looked around the darkened space and thought about her agenda for the day. The reading material had all been utilized and a mural she had started to paint months ago was in the hallway hidden behind mountains of trash. Alice sat down on one of the wooden kitchen table chairs and buried her head in her hands. She closed her eyes and dreamed about walking through the market like she had done on so many beautiful mornings before becoming a prisoner in her fourth-floor walk-up.

Alice remembered the feeling of the morning sun warming her cheeks as she strolled past vendors who proudly displayed their bouquets of colorful flowers. The oversized sunflowers always made her smile and there was nothing like walking home along a quiet side street on a crisp morning with a bag of freshly-baked bread and the yellow petals from the sunflowers peeking over the edge of the paper brown bag.

It seemed like another lifetime when she would freely stroll the market and sip coffee in the cozy corner café. Almost overnight, everything changed and forced into the shadows like a disfigured hunchback in a bell tower, Alice retreated to her apartment, barricading herself from everything and everyone.

Left behind like a forgotten doll, Alice's family moved away and never visited. She understood the circumstances but hoped against hope that they would visit her or return to take her away with them.

After a quick daydream, Alice slid her hand against her stomach to rub away the hunger pains. She stood up and opened the small ice box. Since there was no electricity, nothing in the ice box was kept cold. Its sole purpose had become a haven for her last bits of food. She felt around in the dark and her hands moved over what she thought used to be a potato. She could feel its pruned skin, long knobs of growth protruding from it and furry patches of mold. Alice picked it up off the shelf and closed the ice box door.

She rubbed her fingers around the potato, picked off the buds of growth and took a bite. Her teeth sunk into parts of solid, starchiness with a bit of force and easily chomped through the bits of rotted flesh. Alice chewed and swallowed as quickly as she could, allowing the thin wispy mold hairs to slide down her throat, reminding her of the dirt she once ate on a playground as a child. Alice had to swallow quickly, before her stomach and mind caught onto the condition of what she was eating. She needed to keep the potato down and had learned before that nothing was worse than having to re-eat something her stomach had already rejected.

As the last bits of the spud's flesh slid past her tongue, a heavy hand knocked on the front door. She froze and waited for the unwelcomed visitor to go away. She stood up slowly and looked toward the bottom of the door. The light from under the door was blocked by a shadow. She stood quietly in place and the shadow moved on and the thin ray of light appeared back under her door.

Alice exhaled in relief and wiped her brow.

Another knock, much heavier and with more force than the first. The shadow was back and someone wanted in. Alice looked around the loft for a place to hide as whoever was on the other side of the door wanted in the loft as badly as she wanted out of it.

Pounding harder and yelling something she could not understand, Alice dropped to the floor and crawled toward the furthest corner in the room, away from the door. The banging intensified and Alice knew they had begun to kick with intention of knocking it down and invading her sanctuary.

She searched for some place to hide, anywhere. The boxes were all too small and in a loft, there were no rooms to escape to. She felt around in the darkness and her fingers found the blanket her great grandmother knitted. Terrified by the sound of the bull kicking down the front door, Alice threw the blanket over her and as she laid flat on the floor, she kicked a pile of boxes and papers and they toppled on top of her. Just as the last bit of soiled trash camouflaged her under the blanket, the door was knocked open and someone marched into the room, shouting something unfamiliar repeatedly.

Alice laid motionless. She could see through a small hole in the blanket that the man was wearing clean, shiny black boots. Alice held her breath as she watched the boots move around the room. The person knocked over each pile, searching for something.

Doing her best to lay still, Alice quickly realized that the blanket that shielded her from the invader may also have been her downfall. Like tiny hairs sliding up and down her calves, Alice felt the frenzy of the disturbed fleas as they moved across her skin, biting her, excited for a fresh meal. She was unable to scratch and shoo them away.

Every bite felt like forever as the owner of the boots knocked over piles of trash. Dishes crashed to the floor and shattered into pieces. A sharp broken edge from a saucer bounced along the floor and landed near the hole in the blanket, just inches from her eye.

The fleas began to bite harder and more frequently, angry that their home had been disturbed. Alice's legs began to quiver with the urge to itch but she had to remain still. She could feel something cool pool across the back of her neck and slowly slide down toward her chin. The box she knocked over on top of her was filled with urine-soaked clothes and the liquid had penetrated the blanket and began to drip on her skin. Her body cried out to wipe her neck and kick away the fleas but she had no choice. To survive, she had to remain completely still.

Coughing uncontrollably, the invader had taken in a deep breath of the rotted waste strewn across the floor around him. He shouted again as he gasped for fresh air. Even though Alice didn't speak his language, she knew what he was yelling about as he stormed out to the hallway. She knew he had not grown accustomed to the stench like she had.

A small grey mouse scurried toward the open door and the man stomped down hard. Bits of mouse squirted in all directions as though the man crushed an overly-ripe orange.

He stopped to catch his breath and the sunlight from the staircase windows helped Alice see that he was wearing a uniform. The symbol above his breast pocket was starkly opposite of the large yellow star she was forced to wear.

The invader disappeared down the staircase, his cough fading the further down he went. Alice remained frozen under the flea-infested blanket and mound of crumpled paper and waste, too terrified to move. She was unable to escape, unable to run, and unable to join her family and the many citizens of Paris who made it safely to the countryside. As fleas moved across her lower back, Alice waited, listening for the silence to return to the abandoned building. Her skin burned and begged to be scratched but she dared not move and risk being caught. The pain grew unbearable but she knew that if she moved, her fate would be far worse than the feeling of the tiny insects biting and crawling across her body.

NJ TRANSIT

The inseparable college trio hopped aboard the New Jersey Transit Northeast Corridor train after a never-ending day of lectures and roommate drama. As the train compartment doors slid closed, the illuminated "The Next Stop Is" sign in car 7599 changed from New Brunswick to Edison. Best friends since Psych 101 at Rutgers University, Tammy, Melina and April looked forward to a thrilling evening in the city and they couldn't wait until the train stopped at Penn Station. Little did they know, they would never leave the train alive.

Commuters had already filled most of the seats from the Hamilton and Princeton Junction stations. To make each car even more crowded than usual, there was a basketball game scheduled later that evening and most of them wouldn't exit until New York Penn Station.

April looked down the aisle of seats and saw a sea of red jerseys, tired commuters already zoned-out with earbuds in, and a few elderly couples ready for an early night in the Big Apple.

"Let's just sit here," Melina recommended as she flipped a seat down from the wall. This section of train, usually reserved for handicapped travelers, bicycles and people with extra-large luggage, was empty. No one wanted to sit where the train doors opened at each stop. A cold front moved into the area the night before and there was a noticeably different chill in the air.

Tammy and April followed suit, like they usually did, and sat down beside their friend. Melina was clearly the leader of the pack. From Middle-eastern descent, the dyed wave of purple hair was a stark contrast with her olive skin and the rest of her jet-black hair. She wore a faux -black leather jacket with bright silver zippers, zigging and zagging in every direction. The black-pattern leggings stretched from her short skirt down to her purple Uggs. The stone studded out from her left nostril was a real diamond, not a mall kiosk cubic zirconia.

As though they were a gang without fashion-sense, Tammy opted for a blue streak in her hair and her selected outfit matched similarly to Melina's but the clothes laid differently on her thin black frame than the clothes on her friend's more robust body type.

April leaned back against the wall and twirled her finger through the red streak in her dirty-blonde hair. She opted to avoid leggings and her pasty-white legs looked almost translucent in the light of the train car. Her faded green army jacket and crocheted purse only accentuated her frumpiness but for April, this was as good as things were going to get. She had the book-smarts, Tammy had the common sense and sex appeal while Melina had the confidence.

Before they could settle in for the hour ride to the city, a conductor in a polyester black vest, white shirt and black pants stepped in front of them. "Tickets," he said as he outstretched one hand and kept the other close to his chest, clutching his hole puncher.

"Here you go. These are for the two of us," Melina said as she handed two tickets to him. The conductor grabbed them and with the speed of a lightning-branded superhero, his hole-punch clicked to what sounded like fifty clicks, leaving only one clean tiny hole on each ticket.

He then glanced at April and she said, "I need to find my money." She searched through her purse. He stared at her for a bit. The bill of his hat rested on the thin wire rims of his glasses. "I'll come back for you," he said as he walked away. "Tickets, tickets," he said as he walked down the aisle of the car.

Quickly deep in the thick of pointless conversations filled with "likes", giggles and split-end twirling, the trio talked their way past Edison, Metuchen and MetroPark. The train filled with more and more commuters, basketball fans, and a man whose face was covered by his black hood. He grabbed a seat back in car 7489. Oblivious to their surroundings, the friends continued their conversation.

"Remember Canada?" asked April and she started laughing, digging deep into her purse for cash she knew she didn't have. She forgot to tap the MAC at the Student Union before they left.

"I was like, so drunk, I had no idea how I got back to the hotel," April started. "You all just left me in the club."

Laughing and leaning into Melina's shoulder, Tammy said, "You were so wasted."

"Yeah, we should drink like that tonight when we get to the club," Melina suggested.

"No way, the drinks would be a fortune in that place," April said.

Tammy's head moved back and forth as though watching a tennis match.

"Duhh. But I like, used to live around there and its close to my favorite liquor store. At the counter, we can buy the little bottles of alcohol for like $1.25 each. It's the same as having a regular cocktail," said Melina.

April looked down at her saggy crocheted purse and said, "We'll never be able to sneak the bottles inside."

"No, we'll drink them and then go in already lit," said Melina.

Tammy laughed and offered a high-five to the commander-in-chief.

"Oh, I gotta show you this video. It's like, so funny," Melina said as she unzipped a pocket and took her phone out of her jacket. She turned it sideways and she and Tammy watched a video. The lucky passengers around them were treated to the loud volume of the phone. April sat back against the wall and pressed her knees together. She looked like a marionette tossed aside without it's strings.

"Don't worry about the ticket, girl," Melina said to April without looking up from the screen, "I got you covered when he comes back."

"Thanks," April said as she shoved her purse to her side. She was grateful that Melina's dad spoiled his only daughter.

Melina looked up toward the wall beside her and then at the other wall across from her. "It is like, so weird that on this side there is a poster for gambling in Atlantic City while on that side there's a poster for gambling addiction. It's like, duhh."

Rahway, Linden and then Elizabeth. More and more passengers filled the train and for some of the stops, the conductor announced that passengers toward the back of the train needed to move forward to exit due to track maintenance at the stations.

"After the club, we have got to go to the diner. I like, love that place," Melina recommended.

"Oh I love that diner! Those blueberry pancakes are totally what I need," agreed Tammy.

"Remember the pancakes we had in California?" Melina said.

"I remember those amazing towels in the hotel," said Tammy.

"I still have one," April laughed.

Melina was born and raised on a pedestal and to her, money was as easy to come by as the next paper towel on the roll. Her dad gave her whatever she asked for. Tammy was along for the ride and if Melina was paying, she was in. She had money of her own but didn't need to spend it on anything. She was smart and knew how to work her friend. April, not as fortunate in the cash department, relied often on the kindness of strangers and truly appreciated when Melina paid for trips and weekends in New York City. Her scholarship got her into Rutgers and away from a one-bedroom apartment in Pennsville shared with her father and three brothers.

"Girl, you are crazy. But tonight, we are going to party," Melina snapped her fingers.

"We can't stay too late. I do have to work in the morning," April said.

Eyes glued to the phone screen, Tammy quipped, "yeah but your shift doesn't start until eleven. And it's coffee. You pour it into a cup and serve. Easy as pie."

Melina giggled.

"It's not that easy and it's not just coffee," April started to say but quickly realized her friends were focused back onto watching a video from their California trip.

The train doors opened for the Newark Airport and an Asian couple in their mid-sixties boarded. They sat down across from the friends on the last two available seats. The man reached into his inside jacket pocket and pulled out a tri-fold brochure titled "Big Things! Big Sites, Big Apple!"

His wife, clung to their two pieces of mismatched rolling luggage. She had pulled the small hard plastic red carry-on case while he lugged the oversized brown and black flannel-covered suitcase. The woman gripped them both and kept a leery eye for thieves, arms wrapped around the thin plastic handles.

A sea of red jerseys boarded the train and the basketball fans now outnumbered the commuters and on-the-towners.

Melina looked up from the phone, realizing for the first time just how crowded the train had become. With the seats taken, passengers stood in the aisles and surrounded the friends.

"Two more stops and we're there," she said.

"Oh, I have a test next week and I need to read like three chapters to catch up," Tammy moaned.

"Test in what?" asked April.

"Business II," she replied. "I don't even know why I am like, taking it. I don't plan on spending my life creating budgets and stuff."

"I try to always read ahead. I couldn't imagine being behind in Anatomy and Physiology. I'd be lost forever," April said.

"You two take classes I would never even step ten feet near. Humanities is the easy way to go," smirked Melina.

"Yeah but the rest of us need a job after college. Our degree can't just be a check on a list of accomplishments," April said and the moment the snarky comment escaped her mouth, she knew her friend wouldn't appreciate it. She waited for the backlash, or worse, the reconsideration of the money Melina promised her for the train ticket, club admission and the $1.25 for the little bottle of gin, vodka or whiskey that awaited her at Al's Liquors.

Tammy pursed her lips at April and waited for the hammer that Melina was about to bring down on her friend. However, Melina responded, "Yeah, that's true. I don't have to work after college. I am like, going to marry G and he's going to bring in the money. I can't wait to marry him."

The thought of being a bridesmaid quickly raced through Tammy's head and she lost focus on the dig, much like a dog distracted by a squirrel or a car door closing. "You are so lucky. G is awesome. Kevin is good for now but I don't see myself being with him much longer. I give us until the end of the semester. I'll wait until at least after my birthday and Christmas," Tammy smiled.

"Ooh girl, you are like, evil," Melina laughed.

"Maybe I'll find a guy tonight," April said.

"If you don't pass out you mean," Melina laughed. Tammy joined in.

Secaucus Junction. Doors opened and closed and more passengers boarded and got off.

The conductor made an announcement that passengers in the back of the train needed to move up to cars 7599 or higher to exit the train at the next and final stop, New York Penn Station. All passengers must exit the train.

Passengers in the back of the train began to move forward as the train neared the tunnel under the Hudson River. New York was just around the bend as the train passed dried-out mud swamps. One passenger, wearing a dirt-covered black hoodie, snaked his way closer to the front of the line like an impatient car in rush-hour traffic.

"I am getting like so excited, almost there. Can we say party?" Melina slapped her thighs in excitement.

The crowd around them had grown so thick, the friends could no longer see the Asian couple across from them. The tunnel under the Hudson was just ahead and the man in the hoodie was now a car away from them. The other passengers paid little attention to him. His torn jeans, filthy well-worn pair of Adidas sneakers and lack of a shower turned the faces of each person he passed. Eye contact was avoided as he moved passed everyone.

"Here comes the tunnel, girls," said Tammy.

"Did you guys hear about the people who live in the subways? I was just reading online about how there's an entire society who live in the dark forgotten subway stations," April said.

"Yeah right, mole people," Melina laughed.

"Whatever. Out of sight, out of mind," smirked Tammy.

"No, I'm serious. I read that- "April was interrupted as Melina said, "We really need to get you a man. Maybe it'll be the conductor. He never came back for your ticket."

"Let me see the video from Canada of us at the river. It was so funny when that bird attacked those tourists!" laughed Tammy.

Melina tapped her fingers on her phone's glass screen and the new video played. April leaned her head back against the wall and pressed her purse against her chest. She wondered if she would ever get away from her two friends and thought about the direction her life was taking, hoping for a miracle to happen that would change everything.

The sky and cattails outside the windows disappeared and the black walls of the tunnel enveloped the train. As the train headed deeper into the tunnel, the car door clicked as the passenger in black moved into car 7599.

Nearing Penn Station, the train began to slow and the sports fans became rowdy with pre-game excitement. Thoughts of their team winning, gigantic buckets of well-seasoned French Fries and ice-cold beer raced through their minds. They were in their own worlds. So much so, that no one noticed as the man in the hoodie slowly removed a small blade from his pocket. Like a young boy in small town America sliding a stick along a white-picketed fence, he outstretched his arm and smoothly slid the knife across the necks of the three friends. April first, then Tammy and no sooner did the blade slide through Melina's throat was he placing it back into his hoodie pocket. The three young students slumped into each other like deflated Macy's parade floats.

The train arrived at Penn Station as soon as the doors opened, the hooded man in black was the first to exit. As passengers pushed and shoved their way off the train and up the escalator, no one paid attention to the man as he walked to end of the platform and disappeared into his world in the darkness.

Eventually, a conductor made the gruesome discovery in car 7599.

Passengers in Penn Station waiting for their track number to appear on the monitors would soon discover that the 6:45 Northeast Corridor train to Trenton was going to be delayed.

Fortunately for the passengers on the North Jersey Coast Line, the murders would not affect their commute. Unfortunately for the passengers on the North Jersey Coast Line, a man in a black hoodie had boarded with them.

THE HOTEL

Driving. Alone. After 19 years of being together, we have finally reached the end. Who would have thought that this is how we would end? Me so attached and in love with you. I know you loved me too but not as much as your family. Always second. No matter how much I begged, no matter how much I yelled, you were never able to put us first.

And now, with a suitcase in the trunk, packed for a vacation of one, I am driving away. Further and further away from him. I am driving to the hotel we booked months ago in Williamsburg for our family Thanksgiving weekend. I can't take another fight. I can't survive another rejection. You won't break away from your family but have no problem breaking away from me, breaking another promise. This getaway was going to be for us. You, me and our son. And then, it became just me and our son.

As I backed the car out of the driveway, our son could not help but cry. He missed his daddy and didn't understand why it was just the two of us that were going away. He cried out his name. I stopped the car at the end of the driveway and told him to go back inside the house. I told him to grab his backpack with his iPad and stuffed animals and go back inside to his father. I leaned over to the passenger door and opened it. He pushed the seat forward and climbed out of the car. Rain drops began to slide down the windshield. I told him to go and hurry inside since it was raining, a cold November rain. He ran onto the porch and I backed out of the driveway. As I drove away, I could see him still standing there, watching me leave. A suitcase packed for me and my son still left in the trunk.

South. I needed to drive south. Williamsburg was about seven hours away and it was already getting dark. The rain was dropping harder and faster from the sky. For a pre-holiday evening, the interstate was surprisingly empty. My heart raced. My chest ached. The further I drove, my reality sunk in deeper. I could never go back. Nothing was ever going to be the same. Our family would be broken and split apart. My mind raced as my foot pressed on the gas pedal to just above 70mph. Who would get full custody of our son? The dogs? All the stuff? We have so much stuff in the house, who was going to divide it all up? Who cared anyway, just burn it all.

I tried to drive as far as I could but the rain was coming down in sheets. It splashed against the windshield and the wipers pushed the water off the glass in waves. It was getting more and more difficult to see. The rain was too heavy and it was very hard to see the road ahead of me. There's no way I was going to make it to Williamsburg tonight. And somehow, oddly comforting, I had always known this. I was never going to make it to Williamsburg. It wasn't meant to be, just like us.

I pulled off the interstate at the next exit and stopped at the first hotel I could find. A fast food restaurant was right next door but food was the last thing on my mind. Those golden arches were not calling my name. I parked my car and quickly ran into the hotel. The two glass automatic doors could not open fast enough. I was a drenched rat. Luckily, there were vacancies. The attendant asked if I needed a king bed or two queens. Did it matter?

"It's just for one. Just me," I said to her. In exchange for the approval on my gold credit card, she handed me a plastic room key.

"109," she said.

I asked her if there was a place I could buy a bottle of wine. She pointed out toward the front double glass doors and said the liquor store was just down the street. I turned and followed her direction as she spoke. I could only see darkness beyond the glass. What was she looking at? Did she have night vision?

I said thank you, grabbed my room card and headed back out to my car. My feet not able to avoid any puddles in the parking lot, I was drenched from head to toe by the time I reached my car. I really didn't want a bottle of wine. What I wanted, what I needed was a bottle of vodka. The thoughts in my mind would not stop racing and vodka was all I craved right now.

The liquor store was close, thank god. By the register, I was able to get a small jar of olives as well and then it was a mad dash back to my car through the pouring rain. I walked back into the hotel lobby, dripping wet and even more drenched than before. The brown bag, mostly dry, clutched to my chest. I tried to walk by the front desk as quickly as I could. I could feel her eyes on me. On the brown bag. She knew it wasn't wine and she knew I could not wait to open what was behind the paper. She had seen my kind before. The drunk, checking in alone at one of the year's most popular holidays. No family. A sad soul.

I wasn't a drunk and she didn't understand. Who the hell was she to judge me! She had no idea what I was going through, what I was feeling. Feeling? What was I feeling? Anything? Everything? Nothing. As I opened the door to my room, my stomach sank like I was riding a rollercoaster in Disneyland. Emptiness consumed me. I placed the Privacy Please sign on the outside door handle and slipped into my room. I twisted the latch until the door was locked and slid the chain into its secured position.

I turned the hallway light on and looked around. I stood motionless for a few moments and listened to the silence. The rain scrapped at the window like a dog wanting to come in from the back door.

I needed to dry off; my clothes still in the suitcase in the trunk of my car. I opened a closet door and found a white robe hanging by an iron and ironing board and some odd brown comforter stuffed in a failed space bag. I placed the brown bag and its contents down on the bedside table and quickly peeled off my soaking wet clothes. I grabbed them and slung them over the shower curtain rod to dry. The water dripped slowly off them onto the tub floor, sounding like a soldier slowly tapping a drum. Tap. Tap. Tap. I grabbed a towel from under the sink and dried my body off. It felt so good to be dry. Back out to the closet, I wrapped myself in the robe and grabbed a plastic cup from the stack next to the coffee machine.

I sat down on the bed, opened the olives and dropped two into the cup, topping them off with the vodka. The first glass went down easy. Smooth. I needed that. The light from the bathroom and hallway provided enough light for me to see. For the second helping, I added a bit of the olive juice from the jar and then poured in the vodka. I sat back in the bed and leaned against the headboard. My hands gripped the plastic cup as I listened to the rain taunting me outside.

It came to this. No amount of therapy, wishful thinking and vacation getaways could have saved us. I know this now. All our friends had split up and we were the last remaining couple. Everyone thought that we would be together forever. Hell, I even thought that. I believed in the fairytale, right up until I tossed my suitcase into my car and slammed the trunk closed. I knew then that we were over and there was never going to be a way back for us. We were damaged goods. Trust was broken and God knows I have issues when it comes to trust. For years I had to be the tough one, the bad cop, while you got to be everybody's friend; the nice one. When something got tough or too confrontational for you, I was always the one that had to step up and take care of it. I paid the bills, managed the mortgage company for years and took on all the stresses of a relationship for the both of us. Meanwhile, you went on with your days like everything was sunshine and roses. For you everything always worked out just fine. But did you ever stop to think that the only reason why things always worked out so well was because I was the one behind the scenes pulling the strings, doing my best to keep things going? To keep us going. To keep me going.

Yes, finally, after 19 years, after asking and asking you to share the load, I had to put myself first. You promised you would help, be a partner, not just a husband, but you never followed through. You never stepped up. You said you would but you never did and I was the fool that would just go on and keep taking the jabs, keep facing the issues head on.

I took another sip of my cocktail. The vodka warmed my throat as it slipped down.

And now, here I was alone. What would work out best for everyone? A big messy custody battle over our son? You get one dog and I get the other or would you fight for them both? And the house, under water and worthless. Was that worth fighting for? Another drink, this time half the cup.

I exhaled and wondered why I felt so empty. More empty and angry than sad.   The world that I knew, the world that I loved and fought so hard for was gone. And where were you now?   Somewhere laughing with your family and our son. Me, the loser, alone in a hotel room somewhere in Maryland.

I leaned over and grabbed the bottle and refilled my cup.

Laughing. Not even upset that I was gone. Were you relieved that it was over?   Maybe you are not as angry and upset as I am because you had found someone else.   When we were on shaky ground, did you find comfort in someone else?

I took another swig from the cup.

Maybe you did and maybe it was better that you did. Go ahead and move on and be happy without me. You obviously weren't happy with me. Was anyone? After all, you always made me the bad guy. Would any of our friends really care? Are they more your friends than mine? And how about our son, screaming his name at the very end. He would rather be with you than with me. Was that it? Maybe everyone would be better off without me.

I swallowed the last bit of vodka from my cup, leaving the two olives at the bottom.

Maybe it would be better if I was gone. If no one had to deal with me anymore. Maybe I was the terrible person and it wouldn't matter if I was there or not.

I reached for the bottle again but this time, placed my cup on the end table and admired the etching on the glass. The light from the bathroom sparkled as I turned the bottle in my hand.

I had thought about this so much in the past but now, I knew what had to be done. I knew what everyone was expecting and who was I to disappoint. Ending my life. The issues I had before with it was not about how to do it but where to do it. Killing myself in the house would not have been a viable option. I did not want my son to see me. The bathroom at the office was a possibility but then which co-worker would find me and how would that affect them? But here, in this hotel, in this empty room, found by a stranger. What would I care? What would they care? They probably see it all the time. The front desk clerk eyed me as I came back in from the rain. She had seen my kind so many times before. I bet she has her hand on the dial now, ready to call the police to intervene. That bitch.

I got up from the bed and stood at the bathroom counter. I looked at my face in the mirror. My cheeks were blotchy and red, a side effect from the vodka. My allergy to alcohol. My face always became flushed and blotchy when I drank. It was the main reason why I was not able to drink at work. Someone would always be able to figure me out if I had.

I looked down into the sink and slowly poured the remaining vodka down the drain. The aroma tinged my nostrils. I grabbed the bottle by the hand and with one swift motion, smashed it against the edge of the countertop. The bottle split into five or six pieces and shards of glass scattered across the counter and floor. I turned back my head quickly to avoid the fragments that danced off the mirror.

I still held the handle and sharp edges of broken glass extended out like a glass torch. I pulled my wet clothes off the bar, tossed them on the floor and sat on the edge of the tub. This was going to be it. The end. I was never going to see you or my son again. In just a few minutes, everything that I was feeling was going to be over. My pain would be gone and I would finally be free.

I turned my left arm so my forearm faced up and let it rest on my knee. I gently began to slide the sharp edges of my new instrument against my forearm. Gliding back and forth and back and forth. So slowly, taking in the feeling of the glass against my skin. A tear slid down my cheek as I thought about my son and what I would miss. High school, driving lessons, college, his wedding. Grandchildren. Another tear.

I thought about the past and the first time I held him. The first time he walked and the first time he ran to me. More tears. Full out crying now. This would crush him. As a parent, how could I choose to leave my child? But alone, far from sober and very alone in a strange hotel room just before Thanksgiving, what choice do I have? The glass against my skin feels so good. So relieving.

I knew not to slice my wrist from side to side. Most people didn't die from a cut like that. Instead, they would end up surviving with a scarlet scar. No, I would need to slice up my forearm, follow the blue lines under my skin as far as I could go before I passed out. And deep, I had to cut deep or I may change my mind from the pain. But what pain was worse? The pain from everything that I had just lost or the pain from the jagged broken edges digging into my skin and sliding up my arm. More tears. I was going to miss my son. I was going to miss my dogs. I was going to miss- you.

Oh my god, what was I doing? Had I taken my threats and this stupid fight too far? We could fix this, we could fix us, I knew we could. In the morning, I would drive back, back home and hold onto my family and never let them go. What a fool I had been. They were probably out trying to find me, trying to call me. Where was my cellphone? It was on the counter. I needed to call them and tell that I was so sorry and that I loved them. I needed to call them and tell them that I would be home in the morning and not to worry. Everything was going to be okay.

I reached for the counter and began to stand up but was quickly forced back down. I felt woozy and the room began to cloud. The vodka must have been hitting me hard. I placed my hands on the side of the tub to push myself off and as I pushed, the pain in my left arm was excruciating. I saw stars for a moment, actual fuzzy stars and lifted my left arm so I could see why it hurt so bad.

Blood raced down my forearm and dripped off my elbow. The gash from my wrist down to my bicep was unforgiving. I had done it. So much blood. In my drunken fantasy, I had actually dug the sharpened edges of the glass into my arm. I was feeling more lightheaded and it was hard to keep my balance on the edge of the tub.

No, this can't be. I want everything to be alright now. I changed my mind. Someone needed to help me. Oh god, please someone, take this back. That bitch at the front desk must have called the police by now! I slid backwards off the edge and hit my head on the tile. My arm fell across my chest and I was showered with my own blood. As I lay there, in and out of consciousness, a few last thoughts raced through my mind. My son. I will miss seeing him in high school, passing his driving test, college and I won't be there to walk him down the aisle. What have I done? My husband, you. I do love you. I wish I had known how much before. But it is too late. I did it. My heart is aching, both for my family and for life. Slowly, slowly the room grew dimmer and I my eyes became too heavy to keep open. With my last breath, I could feel regret as I faded away forever. Hoping to be found, not alone for long, in this hotel.

ALONE

Andie looked up from her trainee's computer monitor for a few seconds to take in the view. The clear blue sky enveloped the skyscrapers and the wall to wall windows only exaggerated her view. She couldn't remember the last time that the view had been so spectacular, so peaceful, quite the opposite of how her morning was going. She had spent the last three and a half hours trying to train Samantha on Marchant's basic platform, but she was clearly not getting it. Andie clinched her fists and dove back into training the lost cause.

After a few moments of re-explaining a fundamental function in their system, Andie was about to reach her patience limit, a limit that had been tested before with new hires but not quite at the level where she was with Samantha. Samantha seemed to master annoyance. Her mobile phone vibrated at every turn and she constantly needed to relieve an overactive bladder. This pace would place them far behind schedule and at this rate, Samantha would be ready and raring to go in nine months, if that, at an originally scheduled three weeks.

Saved by the bell, lunch time crashed in like a fallen tree blocking a lion from its prey and Samantha was off to the elevator to enjoy her deserved one-hour break.

Andie leaned back deeply into the leather arm chair, trying to find relief from what she considered a wasted morning. She stared out at the tops of the fellow building that stretched toward the sky. Eighty-four floors up and she felt that she was on almost on top of the world, despite feeling deflated from an exhaustive trainee who Human Resources evaluated as an ideal candidate for the forecasting department. The only thing that Andie was forecasting at the moment was the early dismissal of Samantha, a person who found it more important to read text messages about her dog Scruffles and ask questions about company benefits and policies on improving the quality of toilet paper in the lady's bathroom. Apparently, the two-ply paper chaffed Samantha's personal business and with her economy club plus perks card, Samantha felt she could purchase toilet paper that felt like Egyptian cotton.

After a few moments of visualizing tossing Samantha out of the eighty-fourth floor window, Andie noticed that bright blue sky had begun to fade and turn dark rather quickly. Gray and then total darkness took hold of the brilliant sky and she assumed a thunderstorm was approaching. Now under a florescent spotlight, the outside cityscape melted away into the darkness. Suddenly, the sun returned but only to illuminate the darkness with a sliver of magenta. The late morning seemed more like sunset and the recessed lighting above her flickered, struggling to stay on.

Across town, Chris was enjoying his usual daily lunch with a prospective bank client. He downed another Manhattan on the rocks and nodded in compliance of whatever the flavor of the day was saying. Yesterday Chris nodded in agreement of keeping healthcare policies intact for the homeless and today he nodded in agreement to remove the benefits completely. Like a drone, he stirred the overdressed Caesar Salad with his fork and wished for better company and a medium rare New York Strip with duck-fat french fries. His monthly apartment rent and waist line appreciated his current selection but he died a little inside each day.

Glancing out of the windows toward the street as he took a sip of his second Manhattan, Chris noticed how the daylight gave way to a dark, ominous sky. The restaurant seemed brighter, shining a light on his wasted career and delusional disconnected lunch guest. He hoped that Andie's morning had been going better than his and looked forward to seeing her back in their apartment where they would unwind with a glass of Malbec and sigh, enough to fully explain their day.

Andie sat up in her chair and walked to the large floor to ceiling windows. Outside, the dark sky was earlier illuminated by an orange hew. Something didn't sit right with her. Something was going on. The lights on the floor flickered and after battling for power for a few minutes, exhausted, gave up. Enveloped in darkness, Andie turned around and listened to the gasps from the forecasters. The emergency lights shined down in the far corners of the room and the power struggled to come back on, flashing on and off like a cheap dance club she remembered from college.

Something was happening and it wasn't only Andie that sensed it. As the power flashed back on, hoards moved toward the elevators and someone at the front of the pack frantically pressed the down button. Upon the ding of arrival and graceful slide of the opening doors, people hustled into the elevators to get to the ground floor.

Andie picked up the receiver on a phone at Samantha's desk and dialed Chris' mobile phone. After a few short seconds of silence, a fast-busy ringtone blared in her ear and she knew the circuits were overloaded, something was going on and she needed to get to Chris. She looked around and saw the illuminated exit sign for the staircase. As the lights flickered one last time for survival, Andie walked to the door and opened it to the stairwell. As the door closed behind her, the lights surrendered and she was left in total darkness. She reached into her pant pocket and retrieved her mobile phone. Startled, she stumbled with the passcode to unlock it and then turned on the flashlight. Eighty-four flights down would be a long walk, she knew, but it was better than being stuck on the elevator.

She leaned over the edge of the railing and aimed the light from her phone down, revealing only darkness. It would be a long journey down and now, Andie was regretting wearing her new six-inch heels she bought from Barney's over the weekend. Fashion would be the death of her feet.

Alarmed by the sudden darkness, the customers at Chez Roberto's scurried and fled into the streets, some paying their tabs, others fleeing before they offered a dime for Lobster Thermidor and glasses of dirty martinis. Chris' clients were quite put off by the sudden darkness and ominous orange glow that they abruptly canceled the meeting and frantically dialed their driver for a ride back to their elite hotel, only to find occupied circuits just like everyone else below their tax bracket. Chris tried to call Andie on her mobile phone but was unable to reach her. The ice cubes in his glass smacked against his lips as he downed the last drops of his Manhattan and he stood up to begin his quest to retrieve his soul mate only a few blocks away.

Shining her mobile flashlight on the sign for the sixty-fourth floor, Andie had not come across anyone. The stairwell was just as silent as it was dark. Her feet were already killing her and she had no choice but to leave her brand new four-hundred dollar pumps behind. The chill of the concrete steps breached her stockings and flirted with her toes. She continued to shine her light on the steps in front of her as she made her way down floor after floor.

Chris stepped onto the sidewalk and noticed that traffic had come to a complete stop. The usual lunch-time hustle and bustle and had come to a complete standstill and those people rushing from meeting to meeting or trying to grab a quick falafel wrap from a corner food cart, had found themselves unconscious on the sidewalk. Like victims of a Sleeping Beauty curse, people leaned against their steering wheels in traffic in what seemed to be a heavy sleep.

After what seemed to be a never-ending decline, Andie reached the fifteenth-floor staircase and came across someone curled up in the corner. She tapped the person with her toe but the body didn't move. As she made her way down the stairs, more and more bodies draped themselves on the staircase. The air felt stale and a bit chalky, reminding her of Fall as a young girl, suffering from seasonal allergies.

Chris walked three blocks and stepped over several people, passed out, unconscious bodies littering the sidewalk. He stopped for a moment and stared at a taxi that had crashed into a corner intersection light post. The driver had broken through the windshield and his mid-section had been shredded by the shards of glass. His arms were outstretched over the hood and his blood slid down over the yellow paint. The head of the person in the backseat leaned against the window, much like a sleeping person uncomfortable on a long flight. No one walking, no cars moving or honking, Chris tried to take in the scene, totally foreign to someone who was quite familiar with life in the city.

Andie reached the door of the first-floor staircase and she could see the orange glow of light from the lobby. Just like her floor, the lobby was surrounded by floor to ceiling windows. She held her eye up to the small square window and she could see a few bodies on the ground in the lobby, including Earl, the security guard who she had grown accustomed to over the past four years, sharing opinions about The Bachelor television show every Wednesday morning. Earl was sprawled out over the front desk.

Chris stepped closer to the taxi cab and noticed that the driver seemed to twitch, possibly still alive, unlike the countless others that he had come across. "Are you okay?" Chris asked. The driver lifted his head and with empty eyes, pupils hazed over and staring toward the sky, moaned. The driver reached out toward Chris as if he craved a hug, unaware that his spine was exposed and barely attached to his bottom half, covered by bits of tattered clothing and chunks of glass.

Andie slowly opened the door to the lobby and looked around. Everyone on the first floor, including Earl and the person slumped over in the revolving door, seemed to be dead just like the countless bodies she stepped over on the way down from the eighty-fourth floor. The outside light had transformed to a softened yellow and seemed like an ordinary Thursday, almost to the end of a trying week. Andie stepped toward the security desk and dialed Chris' mobile phone but the line was silent, dead like the people around her.

Chris backed up quickly from the cabbie and knew things were terribly wrong. The world around him had become something out of the Living Dead movies and he had to find Andie before more of the lifeless corpses around him woke up.

Andie dropped the phone and looked out to the street. People were lying unconscious on the sidewalk and cars sat still in the street, crashed into each other, front and back, eerily silent. She stepped toward the revolving door and the body slumped over inside. She was about to step in when she noticed twitching and movement from the person trapped inside the glass doors. "Hello?" she asked as she slammed her hand against the glass. "Are you alright?"

The person trapped in the revolving door stood, bracing himself against the glass. Andie could hear moaning and gasps for air like an asthmatic desperately searching for his inhaler. She leaned in closer to speak with the strange man when he suddenly slammed his head against the glass. She jumped back and watched as the man's jaw slammed shut just as fast as it opened, like a Venus Flytrap attempting to capture its prey. The man's pupils were rolled back, predominately showcasing the whites of his eyes. Andie knew that something wasn't right. The man reminded her of a rabid racoon, clawing its way through the glass to get a taste of her.

Chris ran as fast as he could and dodged his way through the sea of the waking unconscious. He needed to get to Andie, he needed to know that she was okay.

Andie stepped away from the revolving door, terrified, but quickly realized that the seemingly animated cadaver was stuck, forcing its body weight against the revolving door in the wrong direction. Andie leaned against the glass windows and watched as unconscious body after unconscious body rose from the sidewalk, walking and moving stiffly like a partially defrosted caveman trapped in a glacier. She leaned her head against the cool glass and tears raced down her cheek at the thought of never seeing Chris again.

Suddenly, Chris stepped around the corner and stood on the sidewalk just across the street. Andie, exhausted but rejuvenated by the sight of him, slammed her fists against the window to gain his attention. She was so relieved to see him and even more relieved when she realized that he saw her too. Chris crossed the street and walked closer to her, the recently awakened unconscious payed no attention to him.

Andie pounded her fists against the window and shouted to Chris that he couldn't use the revolving door. Chris continued to walk slowly toward her, each step taken deliberately and a bit staggered as though something as strong as a second Manhattan on the rocks had compromised the use of his muscles.

As Andie pounded on the windows, the door to the staircase opened behind her. A man, face drawn and eyes rolled back, outstretched his arms and staggered silently toward her. Andie pounded her fists harder on the glass and Chris stepped slowly closer to the building.

Andie leaned her head on the glass, relieved that she and her love would be reunited. Chris reached the window and pressed his face against the glass opposite of hers, legs still walking, unaware of the solid clear obstacle before him. Andie stepped back from the glass and realized that Chris had become something like the awakened unconscious, like the thing reaching for her in the revolving glass doors.

A tear raced down her cheek as she outstretched her hand toward him. Focused on Chris, Andie was unaware of the soulless being behind her, walking slowly with outstretched hands toward the back of her neck.

JOSHUA

The white underside of the toy tugboat floated on top of the water as the suds from the bubblegum bubble bath began to fade and disperse, creating small island chains of soap. The toy captain and his dolphin companion sunk below the water and rested on the porcelain bottom, just beside four-year-old Joshua. The air in his lungs forced out by the rushing water, creating a weight that kept his body just below the surface. His thin, wispy black hair slowly swirled above the drain cover.

Evelyn sat back against the vanity, drew her knees close to her chest and rested her heavy head. The sleeves on her light pink terrycloth robe were soaked and she sat for a moment, letting the water drench her forehead. She shifted her toes across the blue bathroom rug and took notice of how soft it was. Evelyn lifted her head and reached up toward the sink and grabbed the cordless phone on the counter. She held the phone in her palm, pressed the speakerphone symbol and calmly dialed three numbers- 9-1-1.

The voice on the other end answered, "9-1-1, what is your emergency?"

Evelyn held the phone close to her chin and softly said, "I need the police. I just drowned my son in the bathtub."

A few moments later, she found herself calmly sitting on the living room sofa waiting for the police to arrive. The cordless home phone lay on the wooden coffee table in front of her and she slid her fingers along the sleek black screen of her mobile phone. While waiting for the authorities, she sent a text message to her husband that read "Come home now. Joshua is gone. Police on their way."

Her husband, Jake, had called her six times between the home phone and her mobile since he received the message, but Evelyn didn't pick up. She knew he wouldn't understand or be able to comprehend what had happened in their bathroom unless he had seen it for himself and heard. Her explanation may seem improbable, but she hoped he would understand.

The living room windows suddenly lit up with flashes of blue and red, like someone igniting fireworks in the front yard. Evelyn had informed the 9-1-1 operator that the front door would be unlocked, that there were no weapons in the house and that she would be waiting for the police on the sofa.

After a few hard knocks against the front door and announcing their arrival, the police entered the house and pointed their guns in various directions, several aimed at Evelyn. She showed her hands and slowly set the mobile phone down beside the house phone, TV Guide and a small glass bowl filled with pastel chocolate candies.

Evelyn rubbed her cheek with her sleeve, leaving a small trail of water on her face.

Two officers in plain clothes sat down beside her while the rest of the entourage made their way into the bathroom.

"Can you tell us what happened?" Detective Burke asked.

"I drowned my son in the bathtub. He's in there now," Evelyn said. Her voice did not quiver.

Detective Burke and his partner were taken aback by not only what she just said but by how calm and peaceful she seemed.

"Are you on any medication? Did you drink alcohol this evening?" Burke asked her, trying to understand how she could have done something so unimaginable yet be so still.

"No, no nothing. I am a good mother," she started to say and then caught herself, "was a good mother."

"Can you tell us what happened?" Burke asked.

"He was going to do unspeakable things. He had to be stopped," she responded.

"We're talking about a four-year-old boy, right?" Burke's partner asked as he looked at a photo of Joshua framed on an end table.

Evelyn looked at them both and rubbed her wrists, the wet terrycloth had begun to irritate her skin. "I know you won't believe me. I know it won't make sense, but you should, you must believe me that what I did had to be done. I had no other choice."

Burke looked at his partner and then gently placed his hand on top of Evelyn's and said, "just start at the beginning."

Evelyn slid her hands away and tucked them deep into her sleeves, like a turtle retreating into its shell.

"I am not sure where things turned bad, only that they did. You see, I had a dream," Evelyn began as she heard a commotion just outside the front door. She recognized the voice crying out in disbelief. Jake was home and the officers outside were doing their best to comfort and prepare him. He pushed his way into the house and saw his wife sitting on the couch. His eyes were dark red and tears streamed down his pale cheeks as he did what he could to catch his breath. Evelyn reached for one of the candies in the dish, slid a blue one onto her tongue and then jostled three more between her palm and fingers.

"What did you do!?" Jake screamed at her, "What happened!? Where's Joshua!?"

Burke motioned to two officers behind Jake to take him into another room, anywhere away from Evelyn. Jake was erratic, confused and trembling, quite the opposite from the staunch murderess sitting beside him, eating pastel chocolates like she was a guest at her own party. Clearly, he thought, something wasn't right in the situation. Mothers don't drown their preschool aged children in the bathtub and then go on like nothing happened. She was either a psychopath or in shock and he needed answers.

"Please, you were saying something about a dream," Burke said to Evelyn.

Evelyn sat silent for a moment and listened to the sound of her husband wheezing and crying from the kitchen. She knew he would be upset but she knew that if he heard the reason why she did it that he would understand. "I fell asleep on this couch. It had been a long day. Joshua and I had run errands, you know, typical things like the grocery store, Target, a play date at the playground. By two o'clock we were both exhausted and it was time for his afternoon nap. He was a good napper, always fell right to sleep without any fuss. I laid down on the couch and was out like a light." She popped another candy in her mouth and exhaled. Burke could smell the melted chocolate and peanut in the air.

"I had a dream, a nightmare but it felt real, more than a dream- a vision."

"A vision of what?" Burke's partner asked.

Evelyn looked at them both and said, "People were screaming, crying in the parking lot. Gun shots rang out like exploding popcorn. Someone was inside the mall shooting. I could feel that whoever was inside was trying to kill everyone."

"Go on," said Burke.

"Police surrounded the building and I stood in the middle of the panicked crowd but no one could see me. I could hear and see everything. I could even smell the gunpowder in the air but like a ghost, no one could see me. I searched the sea of screaming faces and at first, I couldn't recognize any of them but then I realized that not only did I recognize them but I knew them all. Their faces though, were much older than they are now."

"Who were they?" Burke asked.

"My neighbors. My friends. They were the parents of the children we know in the neighborhood, but they had aged, at least ten or more years. I slid my hands across my face and I could feel that I hadn't aged like they did."

Burke was about to ask a question when Evelyn continued, "and then I saw him. A boy, a teenage boy stepped out of the mall. Hands in the air and his shirt...his shirt was covered in blood. I stared as hard as I could to see who it was. The police rushed up to him and tackled him to the ground. I stepped closer to him. The blood that had splattered across his cheeks smeared as he lay his head on the pavement, face down while the police wrapped his wrists in handcuffs. He didn't speak. He was very calm. Like the faces in the crowd, I didn't recognize him but as soon as he was lifted to his feet, I saw his eyes. I knew those eyes. It was Joshua, my Joshua."

Burke and his partner took in what she said for a moment and then Burke broke the silence. "You had a dream that your son killed people?"

"Not just people but children, I knew children were in there," she answered. "So many people."

"But it was just a dream," he added.

"No, a vision. It was real, a premonition. If it was a dream, I wouldn't have remembered it when I woke up. I wouldn't have been able to smell the gunpowder. A mother knows her son. A mother has a special bond with her child and this was no dream. It was a warning of what was going to happen. It was real."

"But it didn't happen. No one got shot," Burke's partner interjected.

"No, not yet but it was going to happen. My vision showed me the future."

"Have you experienced anything like this before? Other visions?" Burke asked her.

"I knew the moment when my mother had died even before the phone rang. I knew when the candle was left lit one night and was able to quickly act before the flames burned down our home. I don't know where my visions come from, but they are real and what happens in my visions comes true."

Burke and his partner sat for a minute before his partner said, "What happened next?"

"I heard a child crying, not from the mall but from above me. I looked up toward the sky, the crying grew louder, and the sun was so bright. The light blinded me and then I woke up.

I sat up quickly and heard Joshua crying in his room. He was calling out to me."

The officers in the kitchen escorted Jake out of the house. As he was rushed to the door, Jake held his head in his hands and didn't look over toward his wife.

Evelyn tapped the candies together in her hands and continued. "Joshua had always been a good boy. So easygoing, beautiful. But my vision showed me that there was something in him that I couldn't see. I got up from the couch, grabbed my robe and held him. He squeezed me so tightly and I calmed him down. I didn't know what to do. My vision was so clear. I knew what he was going to become...those innocent children."

"You then took him to the bathtub," Burke said.

"Once he settled down and stopped crying, he said he wanted a tubby-time. That's what we called bath time. He loved playing in the water. He could have spent the rest of his life splashing in the water, playing with his tugboat, pretending the soapy bubbles were giant waves." She paused briefly, popped another candy in her mouth and said, "and that is when it became clear that this was the moment. I loved him so much. I could save everyone and at the same time, give my boy what he loved most. He played with the suds and his tug boat until the very end."

Burke's partner shook his head.

"I know you think I'm a murderer. I'm not. I am a hero. I saved those people and my child died happy. It was peaceful. I saved my child's soul and those people. I am a hero."

Burke exhaled and stood up from the sofa. "Ok, it's time to go. We can take a break here, let you rest and continue this at the station."

Burke gently guided Evelyn to her feet, asked her to place her arms behind her back and read her the Miranda Rights as he locked the handcuffs around her wrists. The last candy dropped out of her palm and rolled across the coffee table.

The cool metal from the handcuffs felt foreign on Evelyn's wrists, tight and chaffing as they slid invasively across her tiny veins. As she stepped closer to the police car, escorted by Burke and his partner, she glanced back and took one last look at her home. Red and blue swirling lights ignited the neighborhood and like dancing ghosts, swept across the stucco façade of her front porch.

She kept her head low as the back door of the squad car opened and she was placed inside. Her shoulders, arched and pulled backwards, ached as she sat down. Evelyn leaned slightly forward away from the leather seat to relieve some of the pressure she felt from her restrained arms.

The entire neighborhood enveloped the area around the Granger home. People she knew and those she had never met gazed and gawked in sad astonishment. Some even cried out. Evelyn shifted her shoulders and her robe began to slide a bit. The sleeves, still wet, soaked her skin more. The soft pink-colored fabric had once provided her comfort, now punishing her as the wetness penetrated not just her skin, but her soul.

Evelyn's husband, Jake, sat on the porch stairs, surrounded by detectives and was being comforted by a neighbor.

The tornado of flashing lights burned her eyes and she closed them just as the body was removed from the house. Jake reached up toward the black bag on the stretcher and screamed out in agony.

Evelyn leaned her forehead against the plexiglass cage and two officers climbed into the front seat. The world outside was crying out in disbelief while Evelyn let the coolness from the glass sooth her head. She was convinced that the unspeakable thing that she had done made her a hero and a savior to so many other children and their families.

One voice grew louder, and the cry echoed above the crowd. It grew louder and more intense and as she opened her eyes, she found herself on the living room sofa. The police, flashing lights and neighborhood crowd were gone. She was back home on the sofa. Evelyn rubbed her hands against the sleeves of her robe and they were dry.

Joshua was crying out to her from his room. Evelyn sat for a moment and thought about her vision. Joshua screamed louder so, as his loving mother, she went to him, knowing exactly what to do.

ESCAPE

Sentenced and placed in cages, we wonder how long we can survive in this new home, a place of darkness and never-ending torture.

"What is that scraping noise? What are you doing over there," Charlie asks me, his faced pressed against the bars.

"I'm marking how many days I've been here," I reply.

"And how many would that be," Ralph asked from beyond the solid wall of bricks and mortar on the other side of my cell.

"Uh," I began. "Four days?" I answer. But the truth is, I'm not really sure anymore. I started to mark the wall with my nail as each day passed. Smart huh? I was trapped in a cell without a clock or a window. Was it daytime? Night? Was the moon full or cut in half? I had no idea. The fault in my plan was after a few scratches into the brick, my marks began to intertwine with the previous prisoner's marks. I counted seventy-four. Seventy-four! Have I been here that long? Impossible. I remember food, freedom and I can smell the great outdoors. Grass, trees and especially my neighbor Roxanne. No one smelled liked Roxanne.

But how long have I been here?

I haven't slept and I haven't eaten. How can we? The slop they feed us is nothing like we're used to at home. Pizza. Oh, pizza, how I adore you. The crispness of your crust with the hint of Roma tomatoes on you. And fortune cookies, how crunchy and sweet you taste on my tongue. No need for a tiny piece of paper to tell me where I would end up. Here. Here in this awful prison. Brick walls envelope me and only a fence and bars allow me to see the other prisoners across the hall.

Directly across from me is Charlie. His long blonde, curly hair has gone grey and ragged. He eats the food our guards give him but there is no choice. Eat the food or starve. We need some sustenance to survive on. Nothing like home. Fresh water and fresh food- chicken, lamb, beef, and carrots. This stuff, this slop they feed us; who knows where it came from.

On the other side of my prison cell, on the other side of the brick wall is Ralph. He is much older than I am and he's been here much longer. I haven't seen him but I know his age because his grey hair is falling out and occasionally drifts into my cell.

"Four days?" asks Ralph. That is nothing. I've been here longer than that. "Have you asked Colonel how long he's been here?"

Colonel. How could I forget him? He's been here longer than any of us. Colonel, laying still, motionless, sleeps in the cell at the end of the hall. Not a sound, not even a whimper comes from his direction. Colonel is a brave one. I have only seen him one time. Our captives pranced him by my cell, dragging him beyond the steel double doors. He disappeared for what seemed to be an eternity, only to return, dripping wet, head low and defeated.

What did they do to him? The torture here is madness. Pure madness! What information did Colonel spill? Nothing? Everything? Were we going to die because of his cowardice or survive because of his bravery?

I wasn't sure but I do know one thing. He returned. Yes, whatever happened to Colonel, whatever torture went on beyond those double steel doors, no matter how horrific or terrible, he survived and returned to us. So many others have been dragged from their cells, ropes around their necks, and pass through those steel doors never to return. I stared at those doors and trembled. When was it going to be my turn?

"Soon," begins Charlie in a hoarse whisper. "Your turn will be soon, as will be mine, Ralph's and everyone else's. We will all go through those doors."

"And then what," I ask?

"I don't know. But it is best not to speak of it. No matter what happens, it's useless. We can kick and howl at the moon, but it won't matter," Charlie continued, "When it's your turn, it's your turn."

Trapped. Trapped in this prison and why. What did I do? What did any of us do? One minute we were free, enjoying the basics of life- a warm bed of my own, food beyond the slop they call a meal here and a home. A place I called home. And a family, people who loved me.

The kids! Where are the kids? I have been here so long I almost forgot about the kids! They must know I am missing and are worried sick! What is this place and how did I get here? How do I get out? "How do I get out?!" I shouted.

"Take it easy. Take it easy," Ralph reassures me from beyond the wall. "You'll be okay. We'll all be okay. How many days have you marked on your wall?"

"Four? Eighteen? Seventy-four?" I reply. "I can't tell which marks are mine and which belong to the other prisoners.

"We have been here a long while," Ralph began. "But don't forget, we are still here and we need each other to survive. So many have crossed through those steel double doors and have never returned. We need to stay strong for them."

Ralph was right. I knew he was right. Max, Sheppard and even Austin. All gone. What were they doing to them? Did they make them talk and then dispose of their bodies? It's been days and they haven't returned. Where are they? What did they do with them?

Suddenly, the steel double doors open and everyone grew silent and still at the sound of rusted metal hinges turning.

Two of them enter the narrow hallway between our cells. I can't see their faces; the light is too dim. It's only bright enough to see their boots and their shirts. Untucked and wrinkled. What is the point of tucking in a uniform if you are only hired to exterminate. To end life. Why put forth the effort?

The boots with the torso-less bodies walk passed my cell to the end of the long hallway. Clop, clop, clop. Suddenly, the sound of the shoes grows louder as the guards return to my cell. My head faces the concrete floor but my eyes double-cross me. They look up to catch a glimpse of what is happening.

The boots turn in the opposite direction of my cell. No! They now face Charlie. One of them reaches into their pocket for keys. Charlie grows restless and begins to pace back and forth in his cell, nowhere to run. Nowhere to hide. The guards unlock his cell and quickly enter. Quickly invade. Before he knows it, a rope is tied around his neck and Charlie is being dragged toward the double steel doors. He kicks and pulls and does what he can to survive; to fight the guards. The more he fights the harder the guard pulls on the rope, tightening around his neck. Charlie tries to dig his feet into the ground but it is no use. The slippery cold concrete doesn't help him. They have him. The guards pull the rope again, hard. Charlie gasps for air and coughs as though something is caught in his throat. It is not food. He did not swallow anything. He is gasping for air as the rope presses against his throat.

Charlie eventually stops fighting when he reaches the double steel doors. They open and the last thing I see as they close behind him is a tuft of his long golden hair, float back toward our cells. It drifts in and out of the light of the corridor, hypnotizing as it floats in the air before me. I become entranced and before I know it, I hear a cold hard crash. The double steel doors are closed and Charlie is gone.

"They have him now," says Ralph. "Now we wait."

"Will he return?" I ask.

"There's no telling. Some go through those doors and come back. Others, our lost friends, never come back," Ralph says as he lays in the corner of his cell. His blanket a tattered shred of what it used to be.

I stare at the double steel doors, waiting for them to open. But there is no sign of life. All I can hear is an occasional cry out for help or a whimper in the cell down the corridor. We all try to be brave. But this place, this prison, has taken its toll on us.

I turn and lay down in the corner of my cell on the cold concrete floor. The walls are closing in. My cell looks bigger from when I first arrived and now, countless days later, maybe four maybe seventy-four, my new home seems so small and cramped. The shadow of the prison bars stretches across my cell's floor. A circular rusted drain is in the middle of the floor. No bathroom in here. I've had to relieve myself several times over the drain, otherwise I'd be sitting in my own filth. No privacy. No comfort. A tiny flat pillow mocks me in the other dark corner of my cell, too small for me to lie on, barely enough space to sit on.

I pick my head up again and stare at the double steel doors. Nothing. Where did they take Charlie? What are they doing to him? Torture? Are they making him talk? Are they killing him? Which one of us will be next?

"I see a van. A dark-colored van!" shouts Colonel. "I can hear voices and," he pauses and then "Two more. They got two more."

The prisoners grow restless when they hear this news. How many of us could they capture? Could none of us escape?

There's a crack in the wall in Colonel's cell. The crack is barely big enough to fit a nose but it gives Colonel a way to see the outside.

Footsteps. They're coming closer. Just beyond the double steel doors. Could it be Charlie? The guards were finished with him. He made it. I knew it! The doors open and a guard enters, dragging two new prisoners into our cell block. They look young, meek and helpless as the guard pulls them down the corridor with a rope around their necks. I couldn't see anymore but I could hear them crying. Their new cell doors squeak as they open and the slam hard like a hammer to an anvil as they close.

Everyone becomes riled up and begins shouting at the guard. "Let us out! We want to go home! What do you want with us?!"

"Be quiet!" screams the guard. Some of the prisoners retreat deeper into their cells and stop shouting. A few of them continue to cry out. The guard takes the ropes in his hand and beats them against the floor, lashing the concrete as hard as he can. The sound of the whip cracking is enough to silence everyone down to a muffled whimper. He continues his walk back toward the double steel doors and stops for a moment in front of my cell. I keep my head down low as I lay in the corner. "And stay there!" he shouts at me. He quickly opens the double steel doors and disappears. I know he is gone but I'm too afraid to look up. The cell block remains quiet and still. The guard's gone but his presence clearly remains. The sound of the whip crack still reverberating in our minds.

Colonel breaks the silence. His cell is directly across from the two new prisoners.

"You're in there together I see," Colonel begins, "they must be running out of places to keep us. What are your names?"

There's a long pause and then a voice answers, "I'm Sam and this is Cody."

Cody wasn't talking. The new prisoner is too busy crying to answer. "There there Cody," says Sam. "We'll make it through this. Be brave."

"We're all in this together. We need to stay strong. Do what you are told to do and before you know it, we will be free," Colonel says, trying to reassure them.

The sound of boots returns and the double steel doors open. I look up quickly, forgetting my orders from the last guard. Two guards enter with another prisoner. The prisoner has a rope tied around his neck and they put him in the cell across from mine; In Charlie's cell. How could they use the cell so soon after he...wait a minute? This prisoner looks like Charlie but different. Charlie had long golden yellow hair and this prisoner has been shaved. His color is much darker and he's wet, soaking wet. The guards remove the rope from his neck and push him into the cell. They leave just as quickly as they had come in.

I stare at the prisoner. He looks familiar but, it can't be.

"Yes, it's me," says Charlie as he sits next to the bars in his cell, resting his head against them.

I stand up and try to get a better look. "Charlie? Is it really you?" I ask and as my eyes adjust to his darkened cell, chills race through my body. It is him. It was Charlie but what did they do to him? "Did they torture you? Are you alright?" I ask him.

"Yes, I am fine, now," he answers.

"Go on soldier, tell us what happened if you can," prods Ralph. "You're back amongst friends now and safe."

Charlie let out a sigh and began, "They dragged me to a post. They tied the rope around my neck to the post. I couldn't get away. The more I pulled, the tighter the rope became around my throat. I could barely breathe. Suddenly, one guard held my feet down while another one shaved my hair off with an electric shaver. I tried to kick and get away but it was no use. The guard held onto me too tightly."

I could feel my eyes grow wide and my mouth drops open. It was suddenly hard to catch my breath and my pulse begins to race.

"Then they took a hose and washed me down with ice cold water. I did everything I could to get away from them and the cold water but I was tied to that post. The water from the hose stopped and one of the guards picked up a gun from a shelf and aimed it at me. He was about to pull the trigger when the other guard told him to stop. He told the other guard to put it away and that I should just go back to my cell wet."

"They almost shot you? Did they ask for anything first? Did you give them any information?" Colonel asks as he rubs his hands together in worry.

"No, no questions. No answers," says Charlie.

"Then it was torture, to mess with your mind. They will do this to all of us," says Colonel.

"We've got to find a way out!" Ralph shouts.

"But how," I ask. "You all have been here longer than me. How can we escape?"

But there is no escape. Day after day, the guards open the double steel doors and take us out one at a time. Sometimes we are placed back in our cells and sometimes, like Charlie and Ralph and finally Colonel, disappear forever. Part of me wishes I knew what happened to them but, honestly, most of me doesn't want to know. Were they tortured? Did they suffer? Were they alive?

New prisoners take their place in my missing friends' cells. Brad, Aaron and Chloe are the next victims to arrive. Chloe is the first female among us and the other prisoners go wild at the sight of her. Howling and carrying on.

My cell becomes my new home. Alone. My only human interaction with the guards is when they toss a bowl of food into my cell, onto the cold concrete. Morning and night, the bowl of food is taken and replaced with the same, cold slop. Whether I ate it or not, I'm given a fresh bowl. I lay in the corner and stare at the food. That's when I notice it's moving, actually moving! Is this my imagination? Have I finally cracked? I drag my lifeless body across the floor closer to the bowl and look down at the food. I haven't eaten anything in at least two days. My scratch marks now made no sense. Timeless.

Starving, I look down at the mess of brown lumps and liquid-like chunks. It is moving. A colony of ants moved in and their long trail leads to a crack in the concrete. Ants or no ants, my body needs sustenance. If I'm going to survive this, I need to eat. I dive in, ants and all, and finally eat. My stomach feels queasy from finally having food to digest. Or is it from the live ants trying to escape my stomach? It doesn't matter. I'm so weak. Too weak to make it to the drain to relieve myself. I'm a shadow of who I used to be when I was surrounded by my friends- Charlie, Ralph and even Colonel. Now I lay in my own urine and feces and no one cares. The guards don't care. I don't care. I know my life is near the end. I will die here alone. Brad, Aaron and Chloe, only here a few days, still feel hopeful of escape, but I know the truth. I know what will happen next.

I sleep often, whether it is day or not, I sleep. I don't dare use the small pillow in my cell as it has long been covered in fecal decay. My cell. My hell. I'm forgotten and no rescue is in sight for me. I lay here in the dark, on the floor and try to remember what my life was like before all this. It's so hard to remember. Playing in the sunshine in the park. Did the sun warm me or was it so hot that it burned? Laying on the couch with friends. Were the cushions soft on my body or did the springs stab me all over. Was the taste of pizza and fortune cookies as good as I remember or did it all taste like brown slop I eat now. My taste buds struggle to remember, giving in to anything. My own leg begins to taste good, licking myself so much the hair on my leg starts to disappear.

My cell is going to be my tomb. There is no way out for me. My friends escaped. I would not be so fortunate.

A sigh, alone in a dark corner. I give up. My body gives up.

More heavy footsteps beyond the double steel doors. They open again and I am too weak, too defeated to look up. This time, the guards stop at my cell. I see their boots. I see the other end of the rope, dragging against the floor. They are finally here for me. This is the end. I am ready. As they slide open the bars to my cell, I lay still. I will not fight them. Please take me. I cannot bare this torture another day. Take me, please.

The rope is fitted over my head and around my neck. The noose has never felt so comforting. I am ready. The guards pull me up and lead me out through the double steel doors. The other prisoners call out to me but I am too weak to look back. No goodbyes. No worries. I know what is in store for me.

The double steel doors close behind me and the howls and cries from my friends are muffled. I am taken down a long hallway toward another door with a small window. This must be it. The end. The shower that Charlie spoke about. The end of the line. Will my friends be waiting for me on the other side?

The door opens and the light from the sun burns my eyes. The room has so many windows I cannot see. This is going to be it. I am here to meet my maker. The one who will officially end my life. End the suffering.

"Buck!" a voice calls out. "There you are! Have you been a good boy?"

The voice is so familiar. It takes me a few minutes to adjust- to the light and to the sound and smell of that voice.

"I missed you," the voice shouts. "Let's go home!"

"Home?" I ask softly in confusion. Unsure of what is happening, my mind races. I know that voice. I know that smell. So, familiar. Safety? Home?

My eyes adjust to the light and I see him. Finally.

"Let's go home boy," the voice says as he slips a collar, my collar, around my neck. The collar is attached to a dark-colored leash with white paw prints on it. The guards remove the rope and disappear behind the door with the small window.

I'm taken out of the building through the front door and the fresh air takes over in my lungs. I let out a loud scream and the figure over me rubs my ears and says "I know, I know you are excited. We'll be home soon. I missed you too boy!"

The car. So familiar. My memories flooding back to me so quickly- my couch, the kids, pizza, fortune cookies- oh sweet fortune cookies how I missed your sweetness! My body warms in comfort and safety.

This isn't the end. This isn't a path to more torture. I'm not going to be killed. I'm being brought- home. Home to my bed. Food, comfort and...love.

"I knew it was a long week away," the voice says from the front seat, "but we all missed you."

The car window next to me rolls down half-way and the cool breeze dances between my ears. I can't resist the urge to sit up and bask in the breeze. So good. This feels so good. And so right.

The voice speaks again as we drive home, "You are such a good boy. Such a good dog. I missed you."

AUTUMN DAY

"Eye on the ball! I said eye on the ball!" shouted the head coach to his varsity players on the field. "Come on now, I said eye on the ball!" The Soma Stallions were not having a good season and the coach's pre-teen soldiers in navy blue were not holding the ball very much in this game. It was getting close to the end of the second quarter and it was the Visitors 0, Home 20.

The Hillman Panthers, however, were having a fantastic season, only losing one game so far to Mayville. The coach, wearing his orange Panther jersey, was focused on his boys and supportive as ever. "That's it, keep it moving, keep it moving. You've got this."

It was one of those perfect October Sunday afternoons. The sun was shining, a cool breeze played with the fallen leaves on the grass and the parents at the playing field took out their blankets and lighter coats for the first time since early Spring.

The Soma parents looked just as defeated as their team. Many of them engaged in conversations, ignoring the game on the field. Only a few of them clung to the fence in attention.

The atmosphere on the home side was just the opposite. The Panther parents were all lined up along the fence, cheering on their boys and showing their pride by wearing their orange sweatshirts and jerseys.

"What a perfect day," said Diane, the team mom.

"Oh, I know," agreed Susan as she took a sip from her third Diet Coke. "It's a little cold, but not too bad. The sun is keeping us just warm enough. And we're going to have another win on our hands."

The playing fields were buzzing and the parking lots full. Many of the cars were parked bumper to bumper along the road into the recreation park. In other fields across the park, a fall soccer game was wrapping up and the next teams, all ten and eleven-years-old, were anxiously kicking around a soccer ball. Their parents standing by with folding chairs under their arms, waiting for the first group of parents to relinquish the best viewing spots.

The smaller children enjoyed the playground, more interested in the swings and tornado slide than any of the sport activities around them.

Another touchdown and now the score was Visitors 0, Home 26. The Panther parents roared with excitement and the Soma Stallion coach called out, "Eye on the ball guys, just like we practiced! Eye on the ball!"

The ground rumbled. A faint whistle could be heard in the distance.

"Alright parents, it's time to announce our 50/50 raffle winner," said the announcer in the concession stand. Marty Sims had been the football announcer for over 30 years. His microphone and booth were set up on the second floor of the concession stand building.

The ground rumbled again and the whistle grew louder, closer.

"$36 is the prize up for grabs. And the winning numbers are 5549983. Do we have a winner?" Marty asked.

"I won I won! That's me!" Darlene Bornea shouted. She was tucked under a homemade blanket and nestled into her folding chair. "I won I won!" she yelled out as she waved her little red ticket in the air with one hand and held on tight to the Big Gulp in the other. She placed her extra-large size soda down on top of the Igloo Cooler next to her and un-wedged her rather large backside from her chair. As she stood up, bits of nacho cheese chips rolled off her blanket and onto the grass.

The ground rumbled again and the whistle blew three times, just beyond the trees that bordered the field. It was the 3:00 train that ran through Hillman every day. The maroon, yellow and rusted blue rail cars raced down the track and peeked through the autumn-colored trees.

No one paid any attention to the train. It did not interrupt the Soma parents from their conversations and it definitely didn't stop Darlene from collecting her winnings.

Another play by the Stallions, not so good. "Interception by the Panthers!" shouted the announcer from the booth. "Panthers have the ball on the visitor 20. Number 47, Zach Kelly caught the ball," Marty continued.

The Panther parents cheered and the Stallion head coach ripped his cap off his head and slammed it against his clipboard. "Eye on the ball, Matthew! What have I been teaching you?! Eye on the ball!"

A buzzer rang out from the scoreboard. Half-time. The teams retreated to opposite corners of the field. The Soma Stallion coach berated his team. "Eye on the ball guys! How many times do we have to go over this, eye on the darn ball!"

Meanwhile, the Panther's head coach, surrounded by kneeling pre-teen boys in orange, praised them for doing a great job. "You are doing great so far. We still have two quarters to go so don't get over confident. If we get further ahead, I will give some you JV boys playing time against the Stallions. It will be good for you to learn against their varsity team." The JV players looked excited at the opportunity and the varsity players seemed more interested in chugging water from their sports bottles.

The buzzer sounded again and the third quarter began. Seven-year old Amy ran up to her mother, nestled back under her blanket, becoming one with her folding chair.

"Mommy, can I have a dollar for some candy?" Amy asked.

"A dollar?" Darlene asked. "You don't need candy. I brought plenty of snacks. There are apple slices in the cooler." As Darlene spoke, she continued to chew and crunch down on the nacho cheese chips in her mouth. She scratched her ear with her orange-dusted fingers.

"But I really want some candy. Ashley's mom gave her money," Amy whined.

Darlene rolled her eyes and reached under her blanket. She pulled out a folded-up dollar bill and handed it to Amy. "Now go away, I am watching your brother play."

Amy skipped off to the concession stand just behind her mom and joined Ashley at the counter.

Another play and the Panther's gained 15 yards. "It's 10 and goal folks," Marty announced. One more play. "Touchdown Hillman Panthers!" Marty shouted. The extra point was good and now the scoreboard read Visitors 0, Home 33.

After a few more dropped balls and finally a decent play, the Stallions were making headway on the field. With a snap and a hard throw, their quarterback threw the ball right into the hands of number 33, Dan Jason. It would have been the perfect play except Dan was a Panther.

"Interception!" Marty called out.

Dan zigged and zagged down the field, leaving all the navy-blue jerseys far behind. "Touchdown Panthers! A 60-yard run down the field. Dan Jason, number 33," said Marty. The extra point was good and the score quickly jumped to Visitors 0, Home 40.

The ground rumbled again.   The Hillman parents were cheering and high-fiving each other. The Soma parents were disengaged and too deep into their conversations to notice.

"Come on guys, eye on the ball!" shouted the Stallion head coach.

The ground rumbled even more.

"Is that another train?" asked one of the Soma parents.

"It must be. How many trains pass through this town?" another parent responded.

The rumbling grew and with a thunderous roar, the sky instantly grew dark. By the time everyone looked up to notice, it was too late.

A 737 was falling from the sky, aiming right toward the field. The nose of the plane crashed into the ground and decimated the fencing and goal post first as it slid and carved its way through the earth. The back half of the plane ripped off, twisting and rolling its way through the crowd. The tail end of the plane slammed down, shredding the playground, bits and pieces of swing set and monkey bars flew into the air as though a grenade just exploded.

The front of the plane plowed down the football field and laid to rest in the trees, catching fire and burning the trees that cradled its cylindrical body. As the body of the plane rolled across the field, one of its wings ripped off and sliced through the concession stand; the top of the building launched off its base like a grand slam ball knocked out of the park.   The base of the stand crumbled under the force from the attack. There was no trace of the teams on the field. Jerseys and bodies were thrust into the air, both from within the plane from the spectators on the ground.

People screamed out in horror as they flew past limbs and burning luggage. The navy-blue and orange jerseys that once shined brightly on the field were gone. The boys were gone, swept away in all the carnage. A blood-stained and partially burned orange jersey clung to metallic plane debris in the center of the field. The number 33, split down the middle, waved in the wind like a wounded flag.

The cries and screams of the survivors were drowned out by the roaring howl of one of the plane's engines, disconnected and howling at the edge of the field in the Visitors end zone. Plumes of black smoke billowed into the sky and blocked the light from the sun. The intense heat from the fires melted the paint, tires and metal from the jammed cars in the parking lot.

The parents and kids on the soccer field were thrown to their feet as the plane slammed down but they were far enough away to be spared of its wrath. Panic calls for emergency help were dialed on cell phones. Some parents ran to help, while others stood motionless, frozen at the site of what just happened; their children crying not quite grasping the magnitude of what they witnessed.

At the football field, the few parents and friends that had managed to survive, climbed out from the wreckage, bleeding, injured, many covered in blood that wasn't their own. Many lay on the ground, calling out for help, calling out in pain, in shock, reaching for an arm or leg that was no longer attached, whether it was theirs or not. The heat from the disaster grew and many bodies had fused together. Flesh, luggage, heaps of twisted metal and bodies, both in navy-blue and orange, littered the field.

The fire trucks and police cars rushed to the scene as quickly as they could. Ambulances soon followed and they went to work, searching for survivors and putting out the flames. The heat so intense, they had to battle their way to even get close to the scene.

Hours passed, seeming like days, and the fires were finally extinguished. Rescuers found a few people, mothers and fathers, and children clinging to life. Darlene's chair was a twisted mess, tangled around a tree at the end of the field. She was nowhere to be found. The fencing that once surrounded the field was ripped away from the ground as though an invisible force of nature tore away a loose band aid. The parents and friends along those fences, now gone or found wrapped in its metallic web. The players on the field were gone, swept away as the wave of metal crashed across the field.

More time passed, an eternity for anyone who made it through. More ambulances drove in to the park as others left with critical patients in tow. Helicopters landed and took off with the most endangered souls. The police and firefighters searched among the wreckage for anyone they could find alive; a needle in a haystack.

Miraculously, the scoreboard survived, only partially damaged from flying debris. Still lit up, it read Visitors 0, Home 40 and the final seconds of the fourth quarter counted down. The buzzer sounded and the game had ended on this autumn day.

CHAPTER 16

A giant pimple seized the tip of my nose the morning of my Bar Mitzvah. My new puss-filled friend settled in right at the crest of my nostrils and acted like a guide as I read from the Torah. While being proposed to at the most magical place on earth, I was invaded by a hair follicle infection that covered my entire body. With a new ring on my finger, I felt like Prince Charming wearing Minnie Mouse's polka dot-covered dress. Yes, with anything good comes something equally, if not infinitely more bad, when it happens to be the 16th of the month.

The number 16 has not been kind to me. 6's in general haven't had my back either but the number 16 has always taken the cake. And by the way, have you *ever* heard of a hair follicle infection? *Seriously!*

My friends have countless stories of what happens to me on the 16th of every month. From injury to money issues to arguments to travel problems, the number 16 is extremely unlucky for me. It is because of my strained relationship with the number 16 that there is not, nor will there ever be, a chapter 16 in this book. Remember the 2016 presidential election? Worst experience involving 16 ever!

By not writing a chapter 16, my intent is to in no way cheat you, the reader, out of a chapter. Please think of this missing chapter like riding in an elevator. There is no option to press "13" and yet we don't feel like the hotel chain cheated us when we get off on the 14th floor. Do you ever feel one floor closer to the ground?

Traffic is heaviest on the 16th and even heavier when its's Friday the 16th. I won't fall asleep if the digital numbers on my alarm clock end on 16. I won't even listen to the radio or watch television if the sound is set to 16. And no way will I ever sit in row 16 on an airplane. My husband will tell you that we literally moved to a seat all the way in the back of the plane just to avoid sitting in that row.

I've tried to ignore the number and when I do, wham bam, like a kick in the crotch when the kid slid into third and I forgot to wear my cup, 16 gets me. Driving back home after a long vacation in Florida, I took the wheel to give my husband a break. He preferred to drive the entire time but needed to rest his eyes. After a few short minutes of being behind the wheel, I looked down and noticed that the soundtrack on the cd clicked to the next track- yep, track 16. I looked up and in front of me, a pick-up truck was hauling a trailer overloaded with junk. Out of nowhere, a metal sign spun into the air and under our car. You know, one of those rectangle signs with one of the ever-changing images of Elvis on it. I did what I could to swerve our car out of the way but the sign sliced our back-driver's tire.

An hour later after we figured out where the spare tire was and how exactly to change the bad tire for the new one, we were back on the road to enjoy bumper to bumper traffic in the pouring rain. To this day, 15 years later, I have never listened to track 16 on that cd or any other album I've purchased. I apologize to any artist who recorded an awesome song on track 16.

This book is filled with dark stories based on my fears and if I included a chapter 16, my fear would be that my unfortunate fate with this twisted number would become your fate. Or worse, whatever I wrote about would come to fruition. Trust me, you don't want me to write a story about ordering #16 on the take-out menu on Friday the 16th. If I did, you'd be reading, or worse, experiencing, a fun-filled weekend with the porcelain bowl and your favorite brand of hiney-bumper tissue. And by the way, I just verified with a dictionary that I spelled "hiney" correctly and the according to the Urban Dictionary, it's correct. The sentence to go along with the word read, "Timothy, don't stick carrots in your hiney." I bet Timmy tried that feat on the 16th. Better to reserve the carrots for a different day and stick to dipping them into hummus.

So again, I apologize for not having written a chapter 16 and I wish you the best of luck as you continue reading this book.

If you enjoy what you're reading, please share this book or, better yet, purchase a few more for your friends. If, however, you have 15 friends in mind, that would mean you've purchased 16 books and I recommend you evaluate just how close these friends really are. I'm sure there's one friend who chews their gum like a cow who you wouldn't mind tossing aside.

And coincidentally, I used Elvis Presley above as an example when he gashed our tire on the 16th. For the record, Elvis Presley died on August 16th.

Respectfully yours and avoiding the number 16, and now peanut butter and banana sandwiches until I die,

-the Author

DARKNESS

"I couldn't see it but I felt it was there, always watching me in the darkness. With my eyes closed and half my face buried into my Star Wars pillowcase, I could feel its warm breath sweep across my exposed cheek. The air quickly saturated with the smell of fresh-cut onions and anchovies, reminding me of a drive along the bay at low tide. I knew it was there but I was too frightened to open my eyes."

Toby adjusted himself on the couch cushion and slid his fingers along the throw pillow, feeling the raised fabric of the tropical flower pattern sewn on it.

Dr. Caulfield jotted a few words down on his notepad and crossed his legs, his chair swiveling a bit as he did so.

Toby continued. "Even with a nightlight on, my room was dark, especially in the far corner across from my bed. The longer I laid there, the more the darkness stretched its arms out toward me and took over more and more of the room."

"How old were you when all of this started?"

"I was seven, maybe eight. I convinced myself that it was just my mind playing tricks on me, me being just a little boy learning not to be afraid of the dark."

"Did you tell your parents about this thing in the dark?" Dr. Caulfield asked.

"My mom worked nights so she wasn't around much when it was time to go to bed. My dad and I were close when I was little. He did what he could to protect me. He was just as good at making sure I was safe in bed as he did making sure the refrigerator was always stocked with beer."

"Alcoholic?" Dr. Caulfield asked.

"Functioning alcoholic. I rarely ever saw him without a beer in his hand but he was always there for me, sober or not."

"Did you tell him about the monster in the dark?" Dr. Caulfield asked.

"Yes, and at first he thought I was just having nightmares about the tooth fairy. I was losing teeth left and right and he said that the idea of someone sneaking into my room at night was what was causing my bad dreams."

"And?"

"What I was seeing didn't go away. I told him it wasn't a bad dream. My dad tried telling me happy stories before bed and even sang a few Bob Dillion songs to me. That didn't help. He ended up making a big production about it."

"Go on."

"One night, he sat in a rocking chair and waited in the dark until I fell asleep. I woke up to the sound of him screaming and yelling. I could hear his fists pound against the carpeted floor and when the lights turned on, he was all sweaty, breathing heavy with bloody knuckles."

"He was playing or really fighting something?" Dr. Caulfield asked, making a few more notes.

"Obviously he was play-fighting for my benefit. It was just in the room."

"And did it help?"

"For a while it did help, but then, one night, it came back and touched me." Toby reached for the glass of water on the end table next to him and took a sip. He held the lukewarm glass in his hand for a bit and then placed it back on the table.

"I hate to stop us here Toby but time is just about up," Dr. Caulfield said as he looked at the clock. 6:54pm. "I don't feel comfortable stopping us here but my seven o'clock is in the waiting room."

"And we wouldn't want to keep him waiting. He has probably read through the same outdated magazine over and over again. You really do need to get some updated reading material out there," Toby joked.

Dr. Caulfield smiled. "I'll make a note of that. Here is what I'd like you to try tonight until our next session. When you go to bed tonight and you think it's with you in your room, keep your eyes closed and think about how your sheets feel against your feet. Rub your feet against your sheets and I want you to really think about the texture. Are the sheets soft or a bit too starchy? Do your toes feel cold or are you comfortable."

"Okay and then what?" Toby asked.

"I want you to train your mind to shift its attention away from what's scaring you. When you begin to sense darkness closing in on you, try this exercise and tell me how it helped. You've been seeing me for three sessions now and you said there were other therapists before me. We need to find an exercise that helps rid you of this fear of the dark."

"Again, I don't have a fear of the dark. It's what lives in the dark that I'm worried about."

Dr. Caulfield looked at his new patient and said, "Please, try this exercise and let me know how it worked for you." Dr. Caulfield said as he stood up from his chair and placed an outstretched hand toward Toby to guide him up from the couch.

Toby exhaled in a bit of frustration and said, "Okay, I'll give it a shot but I don't see how focusing on my feet will help this thing go away."

The two men stared at each other for a moment and the clock on the mantle read 7:05. "Please give the exercise a try and we can discuss it in a few days at your next session."

Dr. Caulfield opened his office door and guided Toby out. He looked out and saw a stout man sitting in a corner chair by a small table, reading a copy of a child's bible. Despite the unseasonably warm evening, the man wore thin leather gloves. "Come in Charles, I am ready for you now."

As the stocky man placed the bible down in the exact spot on the table where he found it, Dr. Caulfield couldn't help himself from thinking about Toby. He wished his session with Toby could have been longer. Tonight, was only the third session he had with Toby and already, he could feel there was something different about this case, something he had not experienced before. Dr. Caulfield knew he had helped many people overcome their fears but something wasn't sitting right with what Toby had shared so far. Toby didn't just need help to overcome a fear of the dark, he needed the tools to, almost, survive in the dark.

As Charles stood up from his seat, four candy bar wrappers he was hiding under his backside were exposed. Charles quickly snatched them up and shoved them into his pants pocket. He kept his head down as he walked into Dr. Caulfield's office and said, "I'm getting better. Only one candy bar for every twenty-five minutes that I waited out there."

"Ok, Charles," Dr. Caulfield said as he closed the door, "maybe if you weren't always an hour early you wouldn't have the need to eat four candy bars. Sit down and let's discuss it."

An empty pasta-sauce stained bowl sat next to the clock on Toby's bedside table. He propped himself up on two pillows and he outstretched his arm, remote in hand, and slowly changed the TV channels, one after another. He had watched his round of favorite nighttime television shows and once eleven o'clock came around, Toby did his usual ritual of flipping back and forth to the evening news, a popular cooking show and every channel in between. He was exhausted after a long day at work and an even longer evening at his therapy session. As hard as he was trying to avoid it, he found it more and more difficult to stay awake. The pasta pot on the stove was calling his name but he was too exhausted to deal with that tonight. He could just soak the pot in the sink in the morning and after another long day, he would scrub it out when he returned home from the office. *Tomorrow would be a take-out night,* he thought to himself.

He looked at the clock and the digital red letters displayed 11:30pm. It was time, he couldn't put it off any longer. He had to close his eyes. He tossed one of the pillows onto the floor, turned off the television and laid down. He placed the remote control on the table and it clanged against the bowl. He laid on his back for a few minutes and stared at the ceiling, the fan spinning in the darkness. He couldn't see it but he could feel cool air blowing down and he could hear the rhythmic hum of its spinning blades. In one corner of the room, a soft orange hue lit up a small area of the wall. It was his happy face nightlight. Toby knew it was not quite normal for a man in his mid-twenties to sleep with a night light but it was much more feasible to sleep with a glowing smiley face than sleeping with all the lights on. He thought the neighbors in the apartment building across the way would find him less odd if he turned off his bedroom lights at night like everyone else did.

Toby turned to sleep on his side and looked at the alarm clock. He reached out and aimed the light of the clock away from his face and toward the wall. He noticed how the red glow from the clock and the orange light from the happy face melted together, appearing a bit like the glow from a dying fire.

The rest of the small bedroom was dark and as afraid of what may be in the room with him, he preferred to fall asleep facing the light. With his back turned toward the darkness, it didn't take long before he felt a draft along his backside and goosebumps danced down his spine. The comforter and sheets were not able to protect him from the sound of something breathing in the dark behind him. Toby thought about what Dr. Caulfield said to him earlier. He closed his eyes tight and instead of focusing on the thing in the dark, he thought about how his feet felt under the covers. He slid his feet slowly back and forth and moved his toes around a bit, allowing himself to feel the softness of the fabric. The sheets felt smooth and comforting as he slid his feet back and forth. He noticed how some areas of the bottom sheet were cooler than others and the more he slid his feet back and forth, the more he became entangled in his covers. It felt really good and after a few moments, he realized he was not thinking about anything else in the room. *Dr. Caulfield was on to something,* he thought and he couldn't wait to tell him that the exercise was working.

Toby continued to slide his feet back and forth on the sheet like a metronome, his tempo easing his mind toward much needed sleep. His serenity was broken when something grabbed ahold of his heel. His heart sank, like an elevator dropping four stories at an amusement park ride. The goosebumps that had melted away on his spine immediately dispersed themselves on his arms and across his body. Toby opened his eyes and was too afraid to turn around. He could feel the weight of someone, of something, enter his bed and whatever held his foot, had long thin fingers with sharp nails. The pointed edges just about pierced the sheets, sliding against the top of his foot like the boney edge of a quill.

The smell of fresh-cut onions and anchovies swept over his cheek and Toby's pulse raced. His lungs screamed as he was too frozen, too frightened to breathe.

As quickly as the thing in the dark appeared, it vanished. His foot was no longer restrained; the weight lifted from his bed. Toby quickly reached for the remote control and pressed the green power button. The television flashed on and using the blue light from the screen, Toby flipped around and looked to see what was there. The screen lit up the room and Toby watched as something dark faded away into the far corner. He needed a glass of water. Propelled by fear, the pasta sauce raced up the back of his throat, burning as it reached his tongue. Not wanting to get out of bed and risk placing his feet on the floor, he took a few deep breathes and swallowed saliva to relieve himself from the heartburn. A glass of water from the kitchen or the bottle of heartburn chewable pills in the bathroom would have helped him but he couldn't risk climbing out of bed now.

After three hours of flipping channels, Toby slid back onto his pillow and fell asleep, waking up every so often to the sound of a loud commercial promoting a new car or the latest dishwashing liquid.

The following day, Toby avoided coming home after work for as long as he could. He ran a few errands and, for the first time ever, ate his General Tso's Chicken at Ming's instead of ordering it to go and eating it on the couch in a generic plastic container. But by 9:30, going back to his apartment proved inevitable.

He entered his apartment and tossed his keys down onto the kitchen counter. He looked at the pot, still soaking in the sink and thought that it wouldn't hurt to let it soak for one more day. Toby fixed himself a glass of water and set it down on his nightstand. After his usual evening routine of brushing his teeth, washing his face, putting on his favorite flannel pajama bottoms, and checking under his bed for monsters, Toby climbed into bed and pulled the cream-colored comforter up close to his chin. He decided to sleep with the lights on tonight, regardless of what the neighbors may think. The ceiling fan spun calmly and the cool air it created washed over his face. He didn't feel like turning on the TV. Instead he would fall asleep listening to the sounds of the city outside his window and the occasional knock against the wall or the ceiling above from a neighbor.

Toby fell asleep on his back and after two hours, his loud snoring woke him up. He picked his head up and looked around the room. Satisfied that he was alone, he closed his eyes again but even with his eyes closed, he could see the light on around him, brightness penetrating through his eyelids with a yellow glow. Toby lifted his arm to cover his eyes but just as he did, the light was blocked out as a shadow slid past him. He quickly sat up and looked around the room again but didn't see anything. He sat as still as he could and held his breath, listening. Silence. He quietly exhaled. A spring from under his bed popped and the sounds of the coil echoed below him.

Again, he wasn't alone in his room and this time, whatever it was, was under his bed. His eyes scoured the room for an escape or for something to use to fight the monster with. Another spring popped and Toby's heart sank. The bed jostled a bit and Toby could hear scraping sounds. It was digging. Whatever it was, it was moving, perhaps finding its way through the box spring and mattress. Toby knew he had to get off the bed but he was too frightened. If he placed a foot down on the carpeting, the thing could take a bite out of his ankle. If he peered over the side of the bed, he imagined it grabbing his face and pulling him underneath the bed.

Toby laid still, his heart practically beating out of his chest as he listened to the sound of something digging its way up, closer toward him. With his back pressed against the mattress and his body unable to move, his eyes focused on the spinning fan on the ceiling. He watched how the blades spun round and round and he tried to focus his eyes on just one of the blades, watching it go round and round. A short beaded-chain below the base rocked back and forth and he allowed himself to feel the cool air against his face. Dr. Caulfield's method was working again and he began to feel calm. The scraping noises under him ceased and the room became quiet, sound coming only from the hum of the spinning fan.

He laid there for a few minutes, basking in the silence and happy he made it through another encounter. Suddenly, just below the surface of the mattress, Toby felt a finger slide across his back, from his neck down to his backside. As the finger pulled away, Toby felt the jagged edge from its nail. Launched out of his bed by fear, Toby sprung toward the hallway and ran into the bathroom. He slammed the door shut behind him and climbed into the tub. He gripped the side of the tub and stared at the strip of light from under the door. Shaking, he watched the light until he could no longer keep his eyes open.

The next morning, Toby woke up and his body ached after spending a night in the bathtub. He climbed out, gaining courage by the daylight, and cautiously stepped into his bedroom. His sheets were thrown almost clear off the side of the bed from when he jumped out towards the door. He took a few steps back away from the bed and slowly

dropped to his knees, bending down to look underneath it.
Toby saw bits of shredded fabric dangling to the carpeting.
He stood and flipped the queen-sized mattress onto the
floor and gaped in astonishment at what he saw. Something
had been clawing its way through the box spring and up
through the mattress, leaving a tattered and frantic hole as
if a grenade exploded under his bed. Toby looked down at
the mattress and something caught his eye. A small metal
object clung to an exposed spring and the morning sun
captured it at just the right angle.

He reached out and saved the tiny object from the spring
and examined it in the palm of his hand. *A tiny gold bell?* he
thought. He didn't remember hearing any jingling bells last
night or any other night he was stalked by the monster.
Toby shook the bell and it did not make a sound. He looked
under it and saw the clapper was missing.

At work, Toby found it nearly impossible to be any sort of
productive. He was exhausted and could not stop thinking
about the bell. The bell was the first real physical evidence
that something was in his room but he wondered how he
would able to prove to anyone, especially Dr. Caulfield, that

the tiny bell came from a monster. He needed more proof and he realized exactly what he needed- the monster itself.

That night, before beginning his usual routine, Toby decided to finally wash the pot in the sink as it had waited for him long enough. He then got into bed and flipped channels on the television until eleven-thirty when he pressed the power button on the remote and set it down on the nightstand. He picked up the bell and waited in the dark for his nightly visitor. The smiley face nightlight mocked him with glee as his heart raced. As the time on the digital clock continued to stretch later into the evening, Toby was feeling more and more anxious. He knew he didn't have a plan at all other than relying on his old wooden baseball bat he had tucked away between his bed and the nightstand.

After waiting in the dark for almost two hours, his eyelids began to grow heavy and he found himself struggling to stay awake. He squeezed the bell tighter in his hand, the sharp rim digging into his palm.

He looked at the nightlight and it seemed brighter than it had just a few moments earlier. He then realized it wasn't the nightlight that had gotten brighter, it was the rest of the room that had grown darker. *It's here*, he thought.

Toby felt something heavy press down on the mattress and he knew he was no longer alone in his bed. Terrified that the monster would surely kill him this time but even more terrified that it wouldn't and that it would disappear again, Toby slowly moved his arm toward the alarm clock and slid the bright digital face toward the foot of his bed. The red numbers illuminated his bed and the monster that had been staring at him from the darkness.

Goosebumps prickled from is spine down to his toes and waves of hot and cold washed over him. Toby could hardly believe he was finally face to face with the monster and he could see it, highlighted in the digital red beams.

Two pale grey eyes, glowing like full moons, stared right back at Toby. It's nose long and curved toward its jagged sharp teeth. It grimaced a smile and pursed its lips. Some of its teeth poked through like a bulldog's underbite.

A few scraggly hairs bent in different directions atop its head and Toby could see small tattered wings shuddering close to its shoulders. One wing nearly gone and seemed almost ripped in half. The monster crouched lower to the bed and was no larger than an elf or dwarf Toby learned about from fairytales.

"Who are you? What do you want from me?" Toby asked, surprising himself that he had the courage to speak. His voice sounded dry and rattled with fear.

The monster sat silent for a moment and tilted its head from side to side, answering in a low hollow voice, "I've come to collect what's mine."

Toby opened his hand to reveal the bell and the monster laughed, sounding wet as though globs of mucous clung to the lining of its lungs. It smacked the tiny object out of Toby's hand and the bell flew to the floor. Toby felt the monster's long nails as its hand swept over his palm.

"No, I've come to collect your teeth," it said.

Toby hesitated and asked, "my teeth? I don't understand. Who are you?"

The monster laughed again; mucous dancing from side to side in its lungs. "I've been trapped with you every night since you were eight years old, ever since your father attacked me in the dark."

Toby's eyes widened as he realized his father really did fight something in the dark when he was kid. "But I don't understand."

"It was our responsibility to visit children while they slept, exchanging currency for tiny teeth."

Toby swallowed and asked, "You're a tooth fairy?"

The monster groaned and said, "I was, until you saw me sneaking away into the night. I came back a few times, always exchanging your newly lost tooth for currency. But then, one night, your father attacked me, broke my wings and with broken wings, I couldn't fly. Trapped in your world, my body transformed into the creature you see before you, forced to live in the shadows of the dark."

"I didn't know," Toby said.

"To fix my wings and return to what I was, I need your teeth, all of them," the monster said.

"But my teeth aren't loose. I'm not a child anymore."

"I need them and you will feel the agony that I've had to endure as I rip them from your gums, one by one."

"No, tooth fairies aren't real!" Toby shouted. "This is not real, I'm dreaming this." Toby took his eyes off the monster and looked up toward the ceiling fan, trying to focus on the sounds of the blades spinning around and around.

"You'll hear every root snap and you'll cry out in agony as I rip each tooth from their socket. Your warm, salty blood will drown your tongue and you'll choke on the pain."

"I can feel the cool air against my face. I can feel the cool air against my face," Toby continued to say.

The monster laughed as more mucous stuck to the back of its throat. Suddenly it leapt onto Toby's chest and landed like a bag of sand. In a flash, it grabbed the baseball bat, snapped it in half and jammed the sharp edges through Toby's shoulder blades, pinning him to the headboard. Toby screamed out in agony.

"Yes boy, open wide for me. One by one," the monster said as it's crooked fingers reached toward Toby's mouth.

The following evening, Dr. Caulfield tapped his pen against his chin. He looked down at his watch and it read 6:25pm.

He opened his office door and found Charles in the waiting room, shoving a chocolate bar into his mouth.

"Come on in Charles. We can get started early. My six o'clock isn't coming."

HER FAREWELL TOUR

Amanda Dallas primped and patted her hair in the mirror repeatedly. The amount of hairspray she used could have glued down the entire planet. She puckered her lips and lathered her favorite ruby-colored lipstick on her newly enhanced luscious lips.

As she put down her tube of lipstick, she glanced at the invitation on top of her bureau. She was cordially invited to a concert of Rai Dai, an evening of music and song for a special, exclusive only audience.

Amanda could hardly care less about the music that Rai Dai contributed to the radio music pool but her teenage children were mad with envy that their parents were invited to this concert. When Rai Dai was in Dallas earlier this summer, they were unable to secure tickets to the concert. The robotic ticket-buying system snatched up the seats in sixty seconds and the only way Gloria and Charles could see the beloved pop music sensation up close would be to buy tickets at $600 a pop. Their mother loved them, but we're not talking about twelve-hundred-dollar love.

Gloria's best friends, Regina and Astoria attended the concert and Gloria had to play off her jealousness with another teenage careless quip of "whatever".

Amanda stared at herself in the mirror. She was just as beautiful and stunning as she was in high school, she thought. The thin wrinkles that framed her lips and eyes were covered by the concealer she used and the hair color tone that Ramon used matched perfectly to her memories of her quinceañera.

Several of her friends were also invited to the concert and they were going to use the limousine that belonged to one her best friends, April. First, dinner at Di Antonio's and then front row center tickets to the concert.

Rai Dai, or as Amanda knew her in high school, Ramona Diaz, was a quiet girl, keeping to herself and excelling at art and music, as far as Amanda could remember. She wasn't as popular as Amanda was and frankly, no one was. Amanda was "the" ideal girl in high school, the one that every girl wanted to inspire to be like and the one girl every boy wanted to be with. Chad Dallas, quarterback of the Dallas Bullhorns, was the only obvious match for her then and still is now. He is the auto dealership king of Dallas and he could beat any deal on a Ford for three counties and counting. Her favorite thing about Chad, other than his tight rear end and washboard abs, was his money. His father, the original king, had died unexpectedly and he left his auto dealership kingdom to his one and only son.

Amanda had it all-looks, money, the best clothes, the biggest and most luxurious home on the block, a statuesque husband and two children that were on their way to being as popular as she was in high school.

But how she ended up with two tickets to the exclusive concert of Rai Dai was beyond her comprehension. She wasn't close to Ramona in school. In fact, she vaguely remembered a locker room incident with the cheerleaders and a pants-less Ramona in the showers and something about a toilet stall. It was all in good fun. It must have been water under the bridge. Amanda smirked in the mirror at the thought of being front and center. She puckered her lips and lathered on her Intensely Red lipstick- her signature color.

Her children begged and pleaded to go in her place but there was no way Amanda was going to pass up the opportunity to sit in the best seats in the house, invited personally by a three-time Grammy award winning, 4-time American Music Award winning superstar. Rai Dai was selling out theaters and stadiums across the country and around the world. The superstar had personally invited Amanda and Chad to her concert. The invitation wasn't printed by some stub hub computer or typed by a lonely assistant. Rai Dai had written the invitation in her own hand.

Ramona Diaz wanted Amanda and Chad to be there and how could she resist? Wherever Rai Dai went, cameras followed and Amanda was born for the limelight. The cameras on the red carpet would just eat her up, each flash capturing every inch of her beauty and confidence as she would fan the personalized invitation in the air passed her face. The world would soon know how much Rai Dai loved and adored Amanda, almost as much as she loved and adored herself.

The grandfather clock in the hallway chimed six o'clock and as reliable as the old clock itself, Chad arrived home. He quickly showered, as he did every day after a long day at work, and dressed himself in the sportscoat, shirt and pants that Amanda had laid out on the bed for him. The limousine had begun to pick up everyone else at six-thirty and Amanda and Chad were the last stop.

As Amanda and Chad stepped into the limousine, their children watched from a third-floor window, looking defeated and deflated at any last possible chance of an extra ticket coming their way.

Dinner at Di Antonio's was as expected- rounds and rounds of bourbon Manhattans for the guys and bottles of pink, bubbly champagne for the ladies.   More alcohol than food was served to the large round table of eight guests. Amanda sat next to Alicia, Amber and Alexa, her best friends since freshman year of high school. The four of them, known as the Straight A's, found themselves inseparable and infatuated with beauty and insufferable by others. While some friends unwound with a good game of bridge or a lady's night with wine and good conversation, the Straight A's indulged themselves in everybody contouring, facial rejuvenating and cosmetic enhancing practice in town. The Straight A's made a full day of it, sometimes followed up by two weeks of isolation at home with bed rest until the bandages came off and their newfound beauty finally being revealed to their waiting public.

The limousine arrived at the Dallas Globe at eight-thirty. The concert was scheduled to begin at nine. Amanda looked out at the crowd, shoulder to shoulder on both sides of the red carpet. Camera flashes streamed like angry lightning in a storm and the dark-tinted windows of her car lessened their glow.

The door opened and Amanda was the first guest out of the limousine. As soon as her high-heel touched the velvety-red surface, all eyes and camera flashes were on her. She looked amazing and deserving of Best in Show. Amanda knew that her friends coming out the car behind her were a distant second, third and fourth place. It may have been a Rai-Dai concert, but Amanda thought of herself as the star. Chad outstretched his arm and he guided his wife through the adoring sea of fans and into the Globe.

The lobby was adorned with Rai-Dai banners and posters that hung from the vaulted ceiling, clung to almost any wall surface and draped above the entry way into the theater. A large security agent in a black tuxedo stood at the theater doors. Chad handed the man the eight tickets and the agent quickly reviewed the information and waved the group inside.

The theater was just about to capacity and the first thing that struck Amanda was the fragrant smell of orange blossoms that floated in the air. As she strutted down the aisle toward her front row seats, she could not help but notice the sea of familiar faces in the crowd. She glanced back toward Amber, Alicia and Alexa to see if they had noticed but they were too busy smiling and chatting away with diarrhea of the mouth, sharing how excited they were to be there. Amanda realized that she was surrounded by her former Bullhorn High schoolmates. There was a clique of cheerleaders who smiled and waved at her in unison. She wished the girls were that coordinated back in school. The main portion of the center orchestra was comprised of former jocks and their wives and girlfriends. None of the guys had retained their former firm and lean bodies, obviously peaking in their senior year. Now, they seemed to have shrunk, expanded quite a bit at their waste-lines and a few had lost a good portion of their hair. Their scalps from the bald spots and receding hairlines glistened in the theater lighting. The last fifteen years had not been good to these guys and the ladies they were with acted like eager flamingos, their heads turning quickly from side to side, scanning each row for a better mate.

The rest of the theater was made up, she could only assume, of other people who attended the same school she had for four years. Those people didn't matter as they weren't in the A crowd. Amanda's husband guided their group toward the front row where they found eight vacant seats in the center. A program for the evening lay on each seat. Amanda grabbed her program and sat dead center in the front row. Although the theater was stunning, the floor did not seem as immaculate so she held her Louis Vuitton purse on her lap.

Chad was speaking with Amber's husband about an upcoming golf tournament when an older woman approached. Amanda was quick to notice the woman's dress, off the rack and ordinary like a school teacher. Her flat shoes had seen better days and her hair color obviously came from a box from the shelves of Wal-Mart.

"Excuse me," the woman said to Chad.

Chad stopped his conversation with Amber's husband and looked up toward the woman.

"You probably don't remember me but recently my husband and I bought our car from your dealership," she said.

Amanda noticed the familiar blank, puzzled look on Chad's face. It was a look he wore regularly as the hamster in the wheel between his ears never ran at full speed.

"Oh, I'm sorry," the woman continued and she put a hand on his knee, "you didn't sell us the car personally. It was one of your salesmen, Jeff."

"Is everything alright with the car?" Chad asked, trying to sound concerned and interested.

"Oh yes, we love it, thank you," she smiled. "It's just that it is so great to see a former student become so successful, right before my very eyes." She continued to smile.

Amanda had no idea who the woman was. She would say that she looked familiar but every middle-class woman in Dallas looked like plain old ordinary cattle to her. It was clear that the woman and the wrinkles that drooped over her cubic zirconia necklace had seen their fair share of father time.

"I was your guidance counselor. I helped you with your application to State," she said.

It was no wonder Amanda had no idea who this woman was. She never stepped one foot inside the Guidance Counselor's office, no need to. Her plan after high school was to marry Chad and get rich quick, by any means necessary.

The light-bulb turned on and Chad suddenly remembered the woman. He smiled with acknowledgement and said, "Oh, yes, it is great to see you again. What brings you here?" he asked. Amanda furled her eyebrows at hearing the moronic question and yet, she really wanted to know how this person also received an exclusive ticket.

"I was Ramona's counselor in school. Despite my better advice, she went on to become so famous. I guess not every girl is intended to find a man and settle down. She is more talented than I ever gave her credit for. I suppose she really knew how to sing after all," she smiled and shrugged her shoulders. The woman then looked at Amanda. "Is this your lovely wife?" she asked.

It was bad enough that Chad was engaging with the woman but there was no way she was going to sink to that level. Amanda quickly opened her Louis Vuitton and buried her head almost entirely inside, searching for something, anything.

The lights flickered and the woman said her pleasant goodbye to Chad and walked back to her seat in the rear of the theater. Amanda lifted her head when the coast was clear and closed her purse. The scent of orange blossoms wafted through the air again. She began to feel a little dizzy. Amanda thought she was light-headed from raising her head up too quickly. The glasses of champagne at dinner didn't help either.

The theater lights dimmed and an oversized screen lowered toward the stage. Everyone started clapping as an image of Rai Dai appeared on the screen.

"Good evening Dallas!" Rai Dai began. "My fellow Bullhorns!" The audience erupted in roars and cheers. The jocks mooed like cattle and a few high-fives were illuminated by the projector's beam.

"Thank you all so much for coming. You have no idea what this evening means to me. I have been dreaming about this moment for a long time and I am absolutely smitten that I have this opportunity. Each of you has had a profound impact on my life."

The scent of orange blossoms grew stronger and Amanda rubbed her eye. She quickly looked around the crowd and everyone was fixated on the hometown celebrity on the screen. The theater doors must have been closed as the back of the room was completely black.

"When I was a little girl, I dreamed of nothing else but to sing. I have performed across the United States and around the world and nothing means more to me than to perform for you, right in the place where I grew up," she smiled and wiped away a tear.

"We love you Rai Dai!" one of the former jocks shouted out to the screen.

"I grew up so quickly here," she continued, "thanks in part to everyone in this theater. You all taught me so many important lessons."

Amanda wasn't quite sure what Rai Dai was talking about. They weren't friends and they never hung out. Amanda didn't pay any attention to her in class. She wondered what lesson she could possibly have taught her.

"The football team, the mighty Bullhorns," Rai Dai began as they cheered and mooed, "you taught me to be strong when you set me up on a fake date. My doorbell rang and instead of the boy I was expecting, a pig awaited me on my doorstep, squealing and snorting. It had a note around its neck," she said as she held up a piece of paper and read from it, "from one pig to another. May you find peace and happiness in your bacon paradise."

Some of the former jocks laughed and most of the audience did too, a few others found the event disturbing.

"I need to thank the cheerleaders," Rai Dai went, "who taught me humility. They removed my drawers in the locker room, leaving me there after gym class. My clothes soaking in a toilet."

A few of the audience members laughed but most of them grew silent.

"From a guidance counselor who told me that I was only good enough to get married and have children to the faculty and staff who allowed the bullying to happen year after year- tonight is for you. Each of you has had the opportunity to bully me and make me feel small just so you could feel big," Rai Dai said.

The orange blossom scent became overpowering and Amanda felt even more dizzy and a bit queasy. She looked over to Chad and he looked like he was having a hard time staying awake, his head bobbing up and down.

Low conversations began to spread around the room. A cough. And then another and another with the added sound of wet, warm blood climbing up their throats.

"I have travelled the world and entertained thousands of my fans. Are you all fans of me now? Now that I am famous, now that your daughters want to be me and your son's just want me?" Rai Dai asked.

A louder grumbling took over the theater, more intense coughing and wheezing. The scent of orange blossoms became overpowering. A small group of jocks stood up in the center to leave and as they took a step, they instantly dropped to the floor. More coughing. A few more people tried to leave and they too fell to the floor, motionless, lifeless, their theater chairs flipping up and smacking against the backrests.

The image of Rai Dai on the screen watched them, silently. More coughing overtook her audience with sounds of gurgling and heaving gasps for air.

Chad fell forward to the floor and vomited blood. Amanda started gasping for air and as she reached for her husband, she fell to the floor beside his dead body. The rest of the people soon followed in groups, sliding to the floor or slumping over in their seats, overtaken by the sweet smell or orange blossoms.

The crying, gasping for air and faint moans for help quickly fell silent.

"I am who I am today because of all of you. I will never forget you. Your children will forever love and adore me," Rai Dai said.

Alicia, Amber and Alexa had toppled onto one another, dying in a bloody mess of contoured, newly engineered perfection.

Amanda closed her eyes one final time and the toxic fumes overtook her lungs. As she took her last breath, she heard Rai Dai's voice above her. She was too weak to open her eyes and her lungs stung, starving for oxygen.

"Thank you for coming to my special evening. It was every bit as lovely as I imagined it would be."

The projector shut off. The screen went dark and the room went silent. Amanda released her grip on her Louis Vuitton and her purse rolled onto the floor next to her corpse. Rai Dai's music began to play on the speakers-

> *You gave me my power,*
> *I owe it to you.*
> *Someday soon,*
> *I'll give it back to you...*

PRESTO CHANGO

Presto chango, Malcolm the Magnificent was on top of his game. Better yet, he was on top of the world. His dazzling and mind-blowing tricks skyrocketed him to the peak of magical greatness. Launched out of the shadows of obscurity and landing directly in the center ring, Malcolm found himself as the world's most renowned magician. Playing on the stage in the Toledo Auditorium was his last night performing for a crowd of less than 500. Destined for greatness, the former clown had been invited to perform on the Royal Stage, a performance to be captured on live television in front of millions across the globe.

All Malcolm the Magnificent had to do tonight was get through his routine, wow the crowd one last time, and the world would be his oyster.

Pull a rabbit out if his purple top hat- check! Walk across a bed of nails- ta da! Card manipulation, illusions, levitating over hot coals- easy peasy lemon squeezy. And the finale, juggling chainsaws. The razor-blades danced in the spotlight and all he had to do was catch one by the handle with his teeth as the blades spun dangerously close to his cheeks - amazing! The crowd was on their feet with thunderous applause. He was as good as packed and ready for the next big performance. He was unstoppable, stupendous. Every magician wanted to be him, tipping their hats in his presence. Every woman wanted to be with him, dropping their undergarments to their knees with one look in their direction. The president of the United States was the most powerful man in the free world until Malcolm the Magnificent graced the universe with his presence. The sky was the limit! There was no looking back. For God's sake, why would he want to anyway?

Once only known for petty gags and a rubber rabbit, Malcolm the Magnificent was formerly known as Sherbet. Not Sherbet the Great or Sherbet the Stupendous, just plain old Sherbet. Available for any tiny tot's birthday party or bar mitzvah for the cheap price of $100 per hour, balloon animals extra.

Saddled with a life of unappreciative toddlers, twisted rubber poodles filled with vodka-fueled breath and a car that ran just as well as his failed marriages had, Sherbet saw no way out. No end in sight of a life surrounded by endless layers of cheap supermarket-frosted birthday cakes and the smell of overloaded rubber training pants waiting to be changed. Yes, destined for greatness but trapped in his own hell, Sherbet the clown lived in a pit of despair and no one seemed to be tossing down a rope any time soon.

Had he worked in an office, perhaps he could climb the corporate ladder, maybe even cheat the system and marry his way into fortune by wedding and bedding the boss' daughter. But alas, there was no boss' daughter in the clown world. The closest he came to big jugs and a warm piece of tail was juggling empty milk cartons and pulling a fluffy bunny out of a hat. Desperate horny housewives didn't want a clown. They preferred a blue-colored man loaded with tools to work their pipes.

Perhaps if he knew how to fly a plane, he could become captain and soar around the world. Children would aspire to be him and women would undress faster than a supersonic jet plane to feel the power of flight he held in his hands. The truth was, sadly as he knew it, his only true talent was applying gobs of white makeup on his face to hide the ailing failure underneath. And let's face it, the big red nose didn't do much to mask a hundred years of big-schnoz genetics. The round red ball only seemed like a glaring beacon atop a cell-phone tower.

Sherbet dreamed of so much more. He wished he was the world's most amazing magician, adored by millions and sought after by women, any member of the female species old enough to stop pining over pink princess castles and fairies riding rainbow unicorns. He prayed for any member of the female species that didn't charge him by the hour-cash only and payment in advance like the gas station near his apartment. Sherbet begged the gods to bring an end to all of the annoying children with their themed parties-cowboys, princesses, puppy dogs dressed like police officers and the so popular never-ending sleepless sleepover with kids hopped up on sugar and giggling through the night, probably reminiscing about the torture they unleashed upon Sherbet. "Another balloon animal! Can I have your nose? Are your feet really that big? Are your farts stinky like cheese?" they'd ask. Never was there a compliment or a question about his craft.

The truth was he wasn't very good at anything, even being a clown. Just like someone picking out a mug in one of those paint-it-yourself stores, you know, in their minds they're another Picasso or Rembrandt. However, in reality, the mug ends up looking like it was painted by one of the three blind mice.

Yes, Sherbet had reached a crossroads- either put up or shut up. Shut up wasn't an option but he didn't have the means to put up, that was, until an unexpected yet welcomed visitor arrived late one August evening.

Alone in his studio apartment, burning the midnight oil as he sat at the kitchen table working and reworking a magic knot trick, Sherbet became ferociously aggravated at the complexity of the most basic of magic tricks, that he chucked the stint of rope out the window. "Damn it all to hell! I'd give anything to be the world's best magician. Anything to never have to put that shitty paint on my face and surround myself with those loathsome brats. Anything!" He shouted.

"Anything?" A voice in the air asked.

Sherbet was startled by the strange voice coming from inside his apartment when he was sure, until that moment anyway, that he was alone.

The voice began again, talking so quickly that Sherbet's head began to swim and lap up all the hopes and dreams it promised. It's voice, so soothing yet haunting, like a stranger's soft words inviting a small child into their car to search for their lost puppy. He knew something wasn't right, something was definitely not kosher. But it didn't matter. What it was offering sounded so wonderful, so fantastic, as though it understood every single one of his aspirations. The voice could eradicate life for Sherbet the clown and usher in a new era, a new chance, as Malcolm the Magnificent. Malcolm the Magnificent, words that never sounded sweeter, no matter the cost.

With a flick of the wrist and a John Hancock in blood, the deal was done. Like movie magic before his eyes, the world of Sherbet disappeared around him. Stars and glimmers of light transformed over-sized rubber shoes into size twelve shiny black Oxfords, his rainbow-ridden clown costumes became a dazzling midnight purple tuxedo with sparkling Swarovski crystals on the lapel. The fake rabbit on the floor took its first real breath and climbed inside a purple top hat. Bags of balloons and empty bottles of Kettle One and Three Olive became escape tanks, trunks and crates, filled to the brim with supplies he needed to perform mind-blowing tricks. His large nose reduced to perfection.

Lost in the shock and awe of it all, Malcolm the Magnificent failed to hear the last words from the mysterious voice. *"Once the greatness you yearn for is achieved, my bill will be paid in full."*

Just as sudden as the sun rose the next morning, life as a clown had vanished and Malcolm the Magnificent stepped out onto the filthy street of Avenue D and was immediately washed over with praise and glory. Like a child lost in an enveloping wave at the beach, Malcolm the Magnificent found himself thrust into the world of stardom, immediately drowning in autographs and photo ops. He was in his glory, all without having to free one rabbit from a hat. He looked around at the sea of adorners around him. No toddler or mildly medicated suburban housewife was in sight. The voice did as it promised. That evening, Malcolm the Magnificent would begin his nation-wide Magnificent Magical Tour, from Albuquerque to Spokane, from Atlanta to Toledo, Malcolm the Magnificent was on fire, a comet the world wasn't ready to reckon with. Every show was sold out and every city begged him to stay for encores. With scheduled engagements and a deep desire to spread his fame, Malcolm the Magnificent followed the tide of his roadies. While they loaded his precious secrets onto semi-trucks, he kept the most important secret, the true secret to his success, deep in the back of his mind. Clouded by the prestige he found himself in, Malcolm the Magnificent, somewhere between Tallahassee and Montgomery, forgot about his deal with the devil. Untouchable like a Capone-era criminal, the magician thought he rose above it all, including the deal that faded further and further to the back of his mind.

Now, bowing once again, curtain call number three, Malcolm the Magnificent bowed to the Ohio crowd. The red velvet curtain closing in front of him could not drown out the sound of their applause. *Just wait,* he thought, *just wait until they see me on the Royal Stage and on their televisions. I'll bring my majesty to their very living rooms!*

Malcolm the Magnificent sat down in front of a large mirror in his dressing room, surrounded by tables overflowing with gourmet cheeses, deli platters, caviar and buckets of champagne on ice. The air conditioning, set to 68 degrees, demand number three on his list to theater owners, gently blew throughout the space. The cool-invisible hands gently caressed scores of red roses.

Malcolm the Magnificent, alone after a performance, per demand number four, set his top hat down on the dressing table and gazed at himself in the mirror. "You are the best magician in the world," he smirked. He turned his head to the left, then right. His profile never looked better. "Perfection," he thought. Life could not get any better and then there was a knock on the door. Malcolm the Magnificent opened the door to find two fine beauties who had come to show him their appreciation for an amazing performance. Now, two of Toledo's finest and well-stacked women wanted to take part in performance of their own. With no cash required, Malcolm the Magnificent let them inside to enjoy a ride on his rising star.

After a long nap aboard his private jet as it flew across the Atlantic, Malcolm the Magnificent checked in to the four-star hotel directly across the street from the Royal Stage. The view from his penthouse suite could not be beat. His name in lights so bright they could be seen from the international space station, as dictated by number one on his list of demands. Soon the world would have a view they wouldn't forget either- him, in big bold Technicolor beaming into living rooms mystifying minds as they devoured TV dinners loaded with Salisbury Steak, creamed corn and cranberry cobbler.

Malcolm the Magnificent enjoyed a dinner of steak seared the way he liked it with a side of lobster and drawn butter, drowned down his throat with a bottle of Dom Perignon. When the meal was completed and he was dressed to the nines in his purple-tinted attire, he grinned and bared it through a high-profile visit in his private space. After all, it was the least he could for her. She was the queen. Once the royal caravan departed for the theatre, Malcolm the Magnificent was escorted across the street and back stage.

Television cameras filled the aisles of the theatre and the sold-out crowd filled the seats. The knick-knack souvenir stands in the lobby couldn't keep up with the demand for Malcolm the Magnificent magnets, keychains and life-size inflatable versions of the idol himself. The first item to sell out was a plush white rabbit that popped out of a purple top-hat. Children loved to cuddle with the rabbit as much as their mothers loved to cuddle with their new inflatable dreamboat in a box.

The orchestra began to play and with a long and thundering drum roll, the large red velvet curtains slid back and Malcolm the Magnificent stood where he was meant to stand his entire life, center stage, engulfed in the spotlight. The crowd roared and Malcolm the Magnificent allowed the applause to continue until a producer signaled it was time to begin. Malcolm the Magnificent made a mental note to have that man fired after the performance.

The televised show was to be divided into two acts, with a brief intermission sponsored by a toothpaste or dental floss company. Malcolm the Magnificent wasn't sure who sponsored it but knew it had something to do with dental health.

The first trick went off like clockwork. Malcolm the Magnificent took off his purple top hat and the crowd went wild as he pulled a white rabbit out by the ears. It wriggled and kicked and then jumped down from his hand, hopped around stage and then with one large leap, disappeared back into his hat. Everyone roared with excitement and waved their plush bunnies in the air. Like a model of precision, Malcolm the Magnificent performed card manipulation with close-up magic, illusions with color-changing doves and death-defying escapes from barrels of water and a large glass tank filled with electric eels. The curtain closed on the first act and Malcolm the Magnificent couldn't wait to get back out and wow them with his powers of levitation. The stage-hands quickly cleared away the tank of eels and began shoveling the burning coals onto the stage.

Malcolm the Magnificent went back to his dressing room and relaxed with a glass of Dom and nibble of watercress salad speckled with caviar, number two on his demand list. While he savored the briny flavor on his tongue, a feeling of dread washed over him. The hairs on the back of his neck stood up when he noticed something being written in blood on the mirror before him. Written with invisible hands, Malcolm the Magnificent read the message to himself: *Once the greatness you yearn for is achieved, my bill will be paid in full.*

Malcolm the Magnificent nearly choked on a leaf of watercress and spit it out, hunched over, coughing, gagging, trying to catch his breath. He looked up again at the mirror and the message was gone. He leaned in closer and slid his fingers across his reflection. There was no trace of blood, no trace of the message. He filled a glass with champagne and swallowed it one gulp. "Keep it together, keep it together. You're Malcolm the Magnificent and nothing will ever change that," he said out loud.

A knock at the door and a voice called out, "you're on in three."

Malcolm the Magnificent took a deep breath, another shot of champagne, straightened the tails of his tuxedo and marched out of his dressing room. The world awaited and he blew off what he saw as an adrenaline slash alcohol-fueled illusion. Tonight, was his night and he was damned if he wasn't going to show the world his magnificence. Unfortunately, he didn't know just how damned he was.

With a thundering drum roll and audience filled with cameras and adorning fans, Malcolm the Magnificent was ready to begin his second act.

Malcolm the Magnificent, with an outstretched arm and flirt-filled smirk, summoned a beauty in the front row to join him. The audience applauded as the bosom-heavy woman in the low-cut gown made her way to the stage. Malcolm the Magnificent took her by the hand and guided her to one end of the trail of burning goals. Flashes of orange and amber glowed under the smoldering piles from one end of the stage to the other. He kissed her hand, asked her if she trusted him as he caressed her calves and removed her shoes. She hid her doubt from the cameras, took a deep breath, and let the magician guide her across the trail of fire. With poise, grace and high heels in hand, she made it to the other end, safe and sound. The audience went wild and Malcolm the Magnificent kissed her cheek and directed her back to her seat. He could taste the rouge from her cheek and savored the flavor as he licked his lip.

Malcolm the Magnificent motioned to the camera that it was his turn to cross the coals and beckoned to the stage hands to add lighter-fluid and more coals. Like an erupting volcano, the coals ignited and the patrons in the front row leaned back, avoiding the flash of heat.

The audience gasped as Malcolm intertwined his fingers and stretched out his arms as he cracked his knuckles in preparation for walking across the flames. He slipped off his shoes and as he was about to take his first step, he paused. For a moment, the audience was silent but then they began to grumble. Was Malcolm the Magnificent backing out?

He smiled at them, turned his back to flames, outstretched his arms like the patron son of the lord almighty, and fell back. People screamed and covered their mouths but the screaming was short-lived. Malcolm the Magnificent didn't fall into the flames. Instead, he levitated above as though he was enjoying a relaxing ride on a float in a swimming pool. As though he was being carried across by invisible trust-fall team members, Malcolm the Magnificent made it to the other end of the flames and gently stood up, planting his feet firmly back on the stage. The crowd too was on their feet and he imagined his audiences at home too were up off their sofas and Lazy-Boys. He had performed a magical miracle and no one and nothing was better, more powerful than him.

Malcolm the Magnificent entertained the crowd with knot tricks and guessing people's weight, ages and birthdays. He had one card trick up his sleeve left and then the finale of whirling chainsaws. Malcolm the Magnificent was in the homestretch and eternal fame would be his.

He removed a deck of cards from his jacket pocket and he began to shuffle the cards as he explained to the audience what he was about to do. As the cards slid between his fingers, Malcolm the Magnificent winced as one sliced his finger. He looked down at his hand for a moment and saw a speck of red on the six of clubs. Malcolm the Magnificent was a master at everything, especially card tricks. His concentration was broken again when another card sliced another finger. Malcolm the Magnificent continued on and tossed the cards into the air. As they floated down, the cards transformed into gold and silver confetti and everyone cheered. He shrugged off the minor accident and continued to the finale.

Malcolm the Magnificent stood at the very edge of the stage, dead center and beckoned the stage hands to bring him five chainsaws. The audience moaned in fear and anticipation as each chainsaw was revved on. Malcolm the Magnificent held three saws in one hand and two in the other. Without hesitation, he tossed them into the air and the blades spun in the air as he juggled them, one, two, three, four and five, round and round, up and down. The chainsaws danced in the spotlight and their smoke from their tiny powerful motors swirled in the air. The drummer in the orchestra began to tap his symbols faster and faster, matching the heartbeats of everyone watching the amazing spectacle.

One catch is all Malcolm the Magnificent had left. One catch, like he had done across America and back again, and he would be remembered as the greatest magician in history. Fame and glory would be his.

The symbols raced faster, children hid their eyes behind their purchased plush bunnies and their mothers buried their faces in the boxed inflatable man candy.

With symbols crashing and chainsaws spiraling in the air, Malcolm the Great opened his mouth and reached up toward the sky to grab a handle. He could see the chainsaw spinning as it dropped toward his face- blade, handle, blade, handle.

The world watched in shock and amazement as the tool spun closer to the performers face. Blade, handle, blade, handle.

With his mouth wide open, Malcolm the Magnificent welcomed in fame and glory.

Blade, handle, blade, handle.

Instead of the handle, the spinning blade end of the chainsaw raced into his mouth. The blades spun and carved through his gums and teeth and down his throat like a carving knife obliterating a Thanksgiving turkey. Malcolm the Magnificent tried to scream but the chainsaw ripping its way down his throat muffled any sound. Chunks of esophagus and tongue flung into the air. The other chainsaws hit the stage around him and danced around in the pools of blood and flesh.

Involuntarily, Malcom the Magnificent's body dropped to its knees as the near-decapitated head flopped toward his backside and his mangled jaw flopped forward like a baby's bib. The sound of the blades ripping through his body sounded like a boot stuck deep into the mud, squishing and suctioning echoing in the theatre. Blood spewed out from his neck, rocketing at the audience like the planned grand-finale of confetti. Everyone screamed in horror and in a chaotic stampede, pushed and shoved to escape the auditorium. The red lights on the cameras showcasing the live event went black as the chainsaw continued to spin and churn inside the carcass on stage.

Malcolm the Magnificent did go down in history that night, earning the greatness he yearned for. The theatre audience never forgot what they witnessed, the home audiences never forgot what they saw live in their living rooms.

The stage hand reached inside Malcolm the Magnificent's body to retrieve the chainsaw, still spinning, still churning inside the performer's body. As the blood-soaked tool dripped down onto to the mangled corpse, the stage hand heard a faint voice say, *"Once the greatness you yearn for is achieved, my bill will be paid in full."*

WRITER'S BLOCK

The small regional airport had seen its share of traffic over the past few months. But, now that the ski season was winding down, the normally busy terminal and the long line at the coffee stand had dwindled down to just a handful of people. Lyle Armister bypassed the luggage carousel. He always had his bags sent ahead before him to ensure they arrived at the lodge and were awaiting him in the room.

He watched as a young lady with long thin black hair stepped up to the counter at the coffee stand. He thought about his favorite cup of liquid energy, a double espresso with an extra shot of caffeine and it had been a long time since he enjoyed one. The clerk behind the register smiled at the girl. Her purple-dyed ponytail swayed behind her as she bopped her head to the jazz music playing on the airport radio.

As the order escaped the woman's mouth, Lyle heard his physician's words in the back of his mind. *Lay low, relax, get away from everything, no stress and by all means, no alcohol or caffeine.*

"On second thought," the young woman said to the purple-haired cashier, "change it to a decaf tea." The barista smiled again and handed her the cup of unsatisfyingly appropriate flavored hot water. Lyle noticed how the string and label of the tea hung over the side of cup, appearing as though the barista forgot to remove the tag from the purchase.

Lyle continued down the escalator and exited the airport through the automatic double glass doors. The air was much colder than he expected, not that he minded all that much. A cold had taken hold of him for years now and he couldn't remember the last time he was truly warm. He thought that by visiting the lodge in late March the bitter cold and snow would have already passed by but it looked like mother nature was as fickle as his soon to be ex-wife.

Only wearing a light spring jacket, Lyle squeezed the collar tighter around his neck and looked down the lane for the courtesy shuttle to his resort. Small mountains of plowed snow hugged the curb. His other hand played with the handle of his worn leather briefcase. The young lady from the coffee stand stepped up beside him and took a sip from her tea. She quickly came to terms with the tea and tossed it in a trash can just a few steps away. Lyle noticed how the tiny white tag fluttered in the air as the cup landed in the depths of the trash can, surrendering frantically like a white flag at the end of an embittered battle. As the edges of the cup disappeared from view, Lyle thought what he would give for a double espresso.

The resort shuttle, normally white and clean, had been battered and stained with the brown and grey slush and sand from the icy roads. The green pine trees painted on the side of the van seemed dirty and not as inviting as the Pine Mountain Lodge had intended. The shuttle stopped in front of him and he stepped aboard. The driver tipped his hat but did not get out of his seat since his passenger wasn't carrying any luggage. Lyle had the pick of seats as the shuttle was empty. *Peace and quiet, just as the doctor ordered,* he thought.

With five rows to choose from, he decided to sit two rows back and by the window, far enough back where he wouldn't have to engage in conversation with the driver and close enough to the front where he wouldn't feel nauseated on the winding road up to the resort. He settled in and exhaled as he looked down at his briefcase and thought about its contents- a fresh bottle of anti-anxiety medication, an unfinished manuscript and a large un-opened brown envelope from his wife's team of attorneys.

Lyle Armister had quickly become a well-known and critically acclaimed author with his first book fifteen years ago, *The Sergeant's Dog*. It was his latest masterpiece though, *Benedict Annie*, that launched him back into the spotlight and onto a six-month book tour around the country. The struggles within his own marriage inspired the creation of his new leading lady, Annie. The public grew to despise her just as much as he and the characters in the book did. Lyle placed his hand on the briefcase and slid his palm across the leather straps. He felt numb about the divorce paperwork that waited for his signature. In truth, he knew the marriage had ended years ago, and the only intimate things that he and his wife had shared was their platinum Visa and Neiman Marcus charge cards. Their marriage had become as plastic and fake as their imprinted names on the cards. She enjoyed draining the money from their account just as quickly as it came in. Lyle could live with a loveless marriage but it was when he learned she was keeping a man on the side in a

Manhattan loft that Lyle knew things had to end. Paying for his wife's desire for high-end labels on everything was something he was content on letting go but paying for his wife's decorator's lavish lifestyle was something he could not get over. The two had become inseparable everywhere except the bedroom. The decorator had a taste for flare and for something she couldn't offer, the God-given appendage between a man's legs. After hearing about Annie's vodka and jealousy-fueled outburst at the Star Lite Lounge on 5th Avenue, Lyle knew it was time to move on to a more stable relationship.

It wasn't the impending divorce that sent Lyle on the verge of a nervous breakdown. Travelling from city to city each night for months on end and forcing himself to smile for his adoring fans was exhausting. Even more, the unfinished book in his briefcase haunted him, the characters left dangling in the middle of a chapter. He was just as unsure of their future as he doubted what had already been written. For the first time in his career, he had writer's block and his characters were not speaking to him. Their dilemmas seemed trivial compared to his own reality. His agent and the public expected so much out of him and ever since the death of his son Jack, Lyle was not able to focus like he used to. A short glass of Jack Daniels on the rocks seemed to help bring things into focus but soon, the effects of self-medicating wore off and he found himself staring at his typewriter, thinking about Jack and the motorcycle he wished never came into their lives. Annie drowned herself in vodka and Chanel curtains and kept their daughter Sophia far from him, away at boarding school. She was growing up without her father and he knew he would hardly recognize her.

Yes, peace and quiet would do him good, as ordered, to get things back into perspective and to calm his nerves. Lyle's doctor preferred that he check himself into a clinic for a short while but Lyle thought that getting away on his own would do him just as good. He visited the Pine Mountain Lodge with his family ever since he was four years old and came back as often as he could.

Lyle's thoughts were interrupted by the sound of heavy feet against the shuttle's steps. He looked up to a see a crowd of women boarding, bags and bags of luggage in tow behind them. For a moment, he had exactly what he needed, seclusion and silence. He hadn't even noticed the young lady from the coffee stand and curb had stepped onto the shuttle as well and had been sitting behind him. Lyle was suddenly thrust into the women's conversation and the group filled the remaining seats on the shuttle. Loud and unaware of him, the women clamored on and their conversation carried back and forth across his seat like cold war nuclear missiles.

"So, Hamilton would absolutely be perfect for Georgia," said one of the screeching voices.

"I totally agreed. She hasn't dated much since things didn't work between her and Sterling but he moved on. I saw him over the summer and Dorit's 40th birthday soiree in South Hampton. He's now with Johanna."

"Is it pronounced Jo-hanna or Joanna? H or no H?" another woman asked, stopping her conversation with the person next to her.

"Johanna with an H. She seemed very lovely, although she kept saying she lived in Royal Falls like she was some debutant but we all know what Royal Falls really means," the woman answered.

"Yes, Queens. The upper crust just seems to be getting a bit closer to the bottom of the pie pan these days. New money," another woman said and they giggled briefly, sounding like boarding school girls from Japan.

Lyle looked up from his seat for just a moment to see what the women looked like. He needed to see who invaded his serenity but he could only see tufts of blonde hair poking out from fur-lined jacket hoods. The shapes of their heads so similar, it was like they were made from the same Westport Connecticut Xerox machine.

The conversation droned on for the thirty-minute ride to the lodge's reception building. Lyle leaned his temple against the window to feel the cold, soothing sensation of the glass. He kept thinking that if the trip had been any longer that he would have been forced to smash his head right through the glass to end the misery. He was a prisoner in the women's never-ending gossiping and chatter with an occasional shushing when someone spoke out of turn.

The shuttle pulled under the lodge's log cabin-like car port at the main reception building, protecting everyone from the snow that began to fall halfway up the mountain. The driver kept the windshield wipers on as he unloaded the sea of luggage. The herd of intruding women exited the vehicle and Lyle paused in his seat and waited as he tried to block out their conversation that continued down the long green carpet and into the resort. It was not until the double automatic doors closed behind them that Lyle had the peace and quiet he needed to reset and begin his long stay. He grabbed ahold of his briefcase and exited the shuttle. A woman wearing a long, heavy black coat stood on the sidewalk. Her white-knitted gloves hugged her clipboard and she tapped her black heels against the concrete, kicking away bits of ice.

"Welcome," she said as she stretched out her hand.

Lyle ignored her and walked by, enduring enough interaction on the shuttle.

"I have your room all ready for you. Just follow me and we can go right there, unless there is somewhere else you'd like to go first," Lyle heard the woman say behind him.

He shook his head no and brushed his hand in the air, shooing her away like an annoying fly.

"Yes, everything you requested is all set and in your room. Shall we?" the woman's voice continued behind him.

Once inside, he was immediately taken back to his childhood. The air in the lodge's great hall smelled like a mix of mulled cider and spiced incense. Large leather couches were arranged around the centerpiece in the room, a roaring fire blazing in the sky-high River Rock fireplace. Lyle did his best to ignore the cackling women to his right at the front desk.

 Except for recent minor renovations still going on around the lodge after a fire, room 3411 was exactly the way it had always been- one king bed hugged the wall on his right and a small dark-stained wooden desk and chair waited for him at the window.

He walked over to the desk and looked through the curtains. The pine trees hugged the mountain all the way to the peak, blanketed in snow just like he remembered. The lake was still frozen and more active than he thought it would be this time of the year. Ice skaters and ice fishermen littered his view. He closed the curtain and set his briefcase down on the desk, beside a bottle of Jack Daniels, a bucket of ice, an empty glass, two packs of white paper and his Underwood typewriter. A small white envelope leaned against the bottle. He opened the letter and it was from his assistant. It read- *Just in case you need to take the edge off. For emergencies, only. With love- Melanie.*

Melanie had been a great assistant and ideal companion for Lyle. She knew what he wanted and how he wanted it even before he did. What he also loved about her is that she did not take any of his guff. If he was irritable and moody, she gave it right back to him and snapped him back to reality. He was really going to miss her. Melanie married her college sweetheart a few years ago, and his job was taking them to Germany. She promised to find him a replacement before she left but to him, there was no replacing Melanie, it was just another loss he had to deal with and eventually come to terms with.

He tucked the note into his briefcase and took out the manuscript, placing it beside the typewriter. He slid his fingers over the keys and decided that a quick nap before work would do him good. Lyle noticed an odor in the room he hadn't noticed when he first walked in, a mix of cooking bacon and a faint odor that reminded him of the time he singed his wrist hair on a candleflame of his daughter's birthday cake when she turned twelve. He thought that his room must have been closer to the kitchen than he remembered. He kicked off his Ferragamo driving shoes and laid down on top of the comforter. He folded his hands across his chest like a corpse and closed his eyes.

Immediately, the sound of herding elephants thumped across the ceiling. He opened his eyes abruptly and the heavy footsteps continued, followed by giggling children.

He folded his arm up over his eyes and tried to fall asleep again but he quickly realized that the elephants upstairs learned how to open and slam drawers and they also loved to listen to cartoons with the volume cranked all the way up.

He decided it was best to just take a shower to refresh himself after his nap and then noticed something else odd in his room.

A once empty luggage rack now supported a dark green suitcase. He stepped closer and slid his fingers along its hard-plastic shell. It wasn't his and he had no idea where it had come from. *Did someone come in while I napped?* he thought.

He tried to open it but it was locked and he didn't have the key. *Definitely not mine*, he thought. Lyle turned toward the phone and was about to call the front desk when he was distracted by the sound of the heard of elephants upstairs. It sounded like they were joined by two heavy-footed sasquatches. He exhaled in frustration. So far, room 3411 was nothing like he remembered.

He waited for the parade of noise to subside and heard their door slam close. Lyle thought that maybe the suitcase had been there the whole time but that he just hadn't noticed, too focused on getting away from those cackling women on the shuttle and finding a place of peace.

The room upstairs had cleared out and he thought now was probably the best time to begin writing and the shower could wait until later. He opened a pack of paper, removed one sheet of paper and fed it to the Underwood, turning the knob gently on his precious antique.

Chapter 7, he typed. He pressed the enter key twice and rested his fingers on the keys. One minute passed, then three minutes and after a few minutes more, more silence from the keys. The page still only read a lonely *Chapter 7. I'll just start typing and see what comes out,* he thought.

Just as he was about to give writing a try, he heard a loud boom followed by the crackling sound of dancing firecrackers outside his window. He brushed the curtain back and could see a small fireworks display going off above the lake. Red, blue, green and purple lit up the white snow and frozen lake. It wasn't as grand as a New York Fourth of July fireworks show or even something children would be amazed at in a theme park. However small, it was distracting enough. Lyle got up from his chair and grabbed the phone on his nightstand and pressed the button for the front desk. He waited a few seconds, listening to the sound of silence on the other end of the receiver. *Renovations must have knocked out the phone lines,* he thought.

Lyle hung up the phone and glanced back at the desk and stack of blank pages. He stepped back by the desk and looked down at his briefcase, the corner of the large brown envelope poked its head out, invading his space. He slid the envelope out and held it for a moment in his hand, shifting his hand as he felt the weight of it.

The lawyers sure have worked for their money on this one. Feels like an Encyclopedia Britannica in here, he said to himself.

He thought about his soon-to-be ex-wife Annie and how things got so bad so fast. He wondered if things were this bad before the death of their son or if things really started to fall apart after.

The sound of heavy footsteps from the hallway echoed into his room, his front door seeming no better a blockade for sound than a paper wall in a Japanese teahouse.

"And did you hear what happened to Madeline when she took those sleep aid pills?" said a woman in the hallway.

"I did, although I can't imagine," another woman said.

He recognized the voices immediately as the women from the shuttle. Lyle walked over to the door and leaned his right eye on the peephole.

"I know. Crapping yourself in the middle of the night, then just laying a clean sheet over the filthy ones and going back to sleep. Truly disgusting," one of the women said.

"I had taken that pill once while on a flight from London to New York. I had two Vodka Stingers and the next thing I knew, the flight attendant was shaking me awake. We had landed and everyone else had already gotten off the plane," another woman said.

"Yes, but at least you didn't soil yourself," a woman added. They giggled a bit and then one of them coughed to urge the other women to behave more civilized.

Lyle could not believe it. The women from the shuttle were in the rooms just across the hall. He watched as one of them fumbled with her room key before finally getting the green light on the keypad.

Lyle leaned against the door and buried his face in the brown envelope. He knew he couldn't work with all the noise, especially knowing that "those" women were just across the hall. They whispered something that he couldn't recognize and he turned and looked out at them through the peephole. They whispered something and were staring toward his room. He pounded his fist hard on the door and like startled schoolchildren, they ducked quickly into their room and closed the door.

Energized by the idea of scaring the Jesus out of them, Lyle became inspired and sat down at the desk, his fingers whirling into a frenzy at the keys.

The wind roared around the lodge and he didn't even notice. It was no sooner that a fresh piece of paper slid against the roll of his typewriter that he was pulling it out, full of typed black letters. With each new page, the thin pages of his manuscript grew and grew. The wind continued to howl louder and the room grew colder.

A few hours later, still active at the keys and finishing chapter 19, he was interrupted by what sounded like thunder.

"More fireworks?" he asked out loud. He looked out through the curtains and expected to see flashes of red, blue and green. Instead, there was only darkness. He looked at the clock on the nightstand and the digital letters flashed 12:00, reminding him of half of the electronics back home in his apartment.

Lyle stretched and twisted his body. He had been writing for a while and had no idea how long he had been working. He looked around the room and suddenly, a tiny elevator dropped in the pit of his stomach. The mysterious green suitcase was opened and sat fully ajar. "Hello?" he called out but no one answered. He searched the bathroom, the closet and even under the bed but no one was there. He stepped back and looked down at the contents folded neatly in the suitcase. By the colors and fabrics of the clothing, he knew the contents belonged to a woman. He looked up on the dresser and something struck him like a knife in his chest. A book sat on the dresser with wispy red yarn stretching out from its middle, marking where someone had been reading it. The coldness overtook his body as he noticed the book's title on the cover- *Benedict Annie, the Final Chapter*.

Lyle could not believe what he was seeing. It was his book, in print and being read by someone. How was this possible? He raced over to the desk and overturned the manuscript to the first page in the pile. Benedict Annie, the Final Chapter by Lyle Armister was typed in bold and centered on the page. He stepped back to the book on the dresser and as he reached to open it, he was interrupted by the sound of a beep as a room key deactivated the lock. The door slowly moved open and the young woman from the coffee stand and airport shuttle walked in.

"What are you doing in here? Get out!!" he shouted at her.

She was holding a small device in her hand and he noticed that she had tiny headphones in both ears. She could not hear him.

"Hello?? You are in *my* room. Get out!" he shouted again as he waved his hands in the air. The young woman did not notice him and slid a backpack off her shoulders. She adjusted an earbud in her right ear and removed a newspaper from her bag and set it down on the bed. She walked into the bathroom and closed the door.

What in the world is going on here!? he asked himself. Lyle looked down at the newspaper on the bed and the tiny elevator in his stomach plunged further down. He could not believe what he was seeing and yet, something about seeing the words in print awoke a truth inside him.

The sound of crackling bacon rang out in his ears and the smell of singed hair and an overpowering campfire engulfed the air around him. The room began to spin and the internal chill he dealt with was quickly replaced with a hot, burning sensation. The glow of orange, yellow and red overtook the room and he found it more and more difficult to breath. Intense heat radiated from the carpet and up through his shoes. Lyle looked down and almost instantly, like paper shriveling into amber dust in the flames of burning logs, the floor gave way, revealing a torrent of fire in the room below. Feeling like a pirate walking a plank above a burning sea, Lyle stood over the flames, balancing himself on a support beam.

He could hear shouting from the hallway and someone calling out "is anybody still up here?"

"I'm here! I'm here!" Lyle cried out. Someone started pounding on the door. "Yes, I'm here! I'm here! Hurry!"

The heat grew more intense and Lyle felt his body cooking above the fire. His skin ached worse than an intense sunburn he experienced as a child. The rubber soles on his shoes dripped into the flames.

Sounding like Vikings ramming a log against a castle's gate, two men in helmets and full gear broke through the door. The flames stretched above Lyle like a tidal wave and the fabric of his shirt and pants fused into his melting skin.

Just as the firefighters stepped inside, the beam below Lyle's feet gave way and he fell into the burning pit below. Looking up one last time, Lyle noticed the tag on the green suitcase, still resting on the luggage rack above him. The name *Sophia Armister* was the last thing he saw before succumbing to his fate.

Sophia stepped out of the bathroom and removed the earbuds from her ears. She sat down on the bed beside the newspaper and laid it on her lap. The headline read *Famous Author Killed in Lodge Fire*.

She stood up and walked to the desk where she grabbed the bottle of Jack Daniels and poured a bit into a glass. Sophia raised the glass toward the Underwood. "Here's to you, Dad. I'll come back every year."

A few months passed and the small regional airport had seen its share of traffic over the past few months but now that the ski season was winding down, the normally busy terminal and the long line at the coffee stand had dwindled down to just a handful of people. Lyle Armister bypassed the luggage carousel. He always had his bags sent ahead before him to ensure they arrived at the lodge and were awaiting him in the room.

He watched as a young lady with long thin black hair stepped up to the counter at the coffee stand. He thought about his favorite cup of liquid energy, a double espresso with an extra shot of caffeine and it had been a long time since he enjoyed one.

WHITE SANDS

White Sands was set to be the premier community nestled between Orlando and Davenport Florida. Hugging Interstate 4, the planned community was to be the ideal escape for people working for an entertaining mouse, an acrobatic Killer Whale or at a theme park filled with an eclectic collection of movie characters. Starting from the mid 200's, buyers had the option of selecting between one of five model homes with a half-dozen exterior color options.

Regardless of the type of home built on the lot, landscaping was designed to be uniform and tidy with one Magnolia tree in each backyard and general green foliage and red mulch to border the pathway to each front door. Roystonea Palms were planted in front of each house so eventually, when each tree outgrew its supportive wire and wooden support-stakes, the streets would be lined by rows or beautiful towering palms.

Unfortunately, due to a viscous international trade war between the United States and several other world super powers followed by a recession a few years later, things in White Sands did not go as planned. Five homes lined a street along one edge of the community but every other block was peppered with just one home or a home with a partially constructed one next to it. For the most part, White Sands consisted of sand lots with white and blue pvc pipes sprouting out from jungles of weeds or slabs of concrete with partially constructed walls, abandoned and left without a roof. The only remains of what was supposed to be the community pool and clubhouse was a sign nailed to the side of a portable toilet. The plastic door swung open in the breeze and the Florida sun reflected off the sign on the door- "Pete's Portable Johns. When nature calls, have a seat on us."

The homes that were built looked pristine and perfect. The palms were growing as planned and the Magnolias were blooming as hoped. Everything on the outside looked as it should be. The house on Everett Way looked just like three other houses in the community- beige stucco exterior walls with white trim and an SUV parked in the driveway.

However, inside this house things were very different than anyone could have ever imagined.

Maggy James and her four siblings moved to White Sands three years earlier. Their parents had taken the family from Knoxville when they inherited a large sum of money after Maggy's grandmother passed away. Never allowed out of the house, the five James children lived in fear of their parents. Their parents supplied just enough food for the children to survive and the kids learned to make clothes out of the scraps their mother brought home from the fabric store. While their parents would go out in the evening for high-end dinners, the children would be shackled to bed posts, the chains just long enough to reach the bathroom toilet. The doors and windows always remained locked and the security system armed.

The children hadn't been outside since they moved to White Sands. In a development with hardly any neighbors, 114 Everett Way was the ideal cover to hide the five children away from the rest of the world. Their only means of escape out of the torturous life they knew was to use their imaginations and play with what little toys they had.

No one ever knows what goes on inside pretty homes on a palm tree-lined street just beyond the lands of miniature golf, amusement rides and funnel cakes. Appearances on the outside are not always what they seem, whether it's a house or a person.

Maggie, while pulling on the shackle that gripped her ankle, discovered a power that seemed like a dream but would later prove...

Stay tuned to find out what happens to Maggie and the rest of the characters who regrettably found their way into the next book of short stories and tales of horror by Andrew Kraus.

ABOUT THE AUTHOR

Andrew Kraus is a novelist with a penchant for the more melancholy side of life. His fascination with the supernatural, otherworldly and ethereal began in early childhood. When other children were watching cartoons, he was studying horror films. As a young man, when others were riding roller coasters, he was heading to haunted attractions for decorating tips. And now, as an adult, when searching for a home, his preference is for something haunted.

Andrew currently resides in a turn of the century Victorian style farm house in southern New Jersey with his husband, their son, three dogs, and at minimum four spirits. Andrew finds that his home and the spirits within give him inspiration to put pen to paper and share the stories of terror, tragedy, and misery that flow from his cranium. When he isn't writing, he and his family love to travel the globe in search of the macabre.